*"Should I consider this a pass?" Mac asked eagerly. "Or are we going to neck in the line of duty?"*

"Put your arm around me, you Casanova, and save your line for your regular dates." Kate whispered into his ear. "But if you kiss me, you'll be sore for a week."

His head bent to the warm place where her neck joined her shoulder. "You smell sweet." Then, in a sudden move, he pulled her hard against him, and her heart began beating in a crazy rhythm.

"Don't worry, Kate, you know it's just business," he murmured into her hair. She relaxed in his arms, and he chose that moment to haul her into his lap.

"MacHugh, you are the most—"

"Now you'll have to kiss me," he told her, smiling. "That guy watching can see us better like this." Kate checked the man they'd been trailing, and in a moment of inattention, Mac took charge for good.

His lips pressed against hers, warm and soft, gentle but persuasive, and soon Kate forgot everything but the hands that held her close, the heart beating next to hers, and the mouth that knew how to answer her secret longings. . . .

## WHAT ARE *LOVESWEPT* ROMANCES?

They are stories of true romance and touching emotion. We believe those two very important ingredients are constants in our highly sensual and very believable stories in the *LOVESWEPT* line. Our goal is to give you, the reader, stories of consistently high quality that may sometimes make you laugh, sometimes make you cry, but are always fresh and creative and contain many delightful surprises within their pages.

Most romance fans read an enormous number of books. Those they truly love, they keep. Others may be traded with friends and soon forgotten. We hope that each *LOVESWEPT* romance will be a treasure—a "keeper." We will always try to publish

*LOVE STORIES YOU'LL NEVER FORGET*
*BY AUTHORS YOU'LL ALWAYS REMEMBER*

The Editors

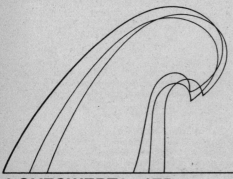

**LOVESWEPT® • 175**

# Kimberli Wagner
# Exposé

 **BANTAM BOOKS**
**TORONTO • NEW YORK • LONDON • SYDNEY • AUCKLAND**

**For**
**Elsie Cromwell, Jane Gordon,**
**Ian Gordon and Elsie Lee**
**with love**

EXPOSÉ
*A Bantam Book / January 1987*

If you would be interested in receiving protective vinyl
covers for your Loveswept books, please write to this address
for information:

Loveswept
Bantam Books
P.O. Box 985
Hicksville, NY 11802

ISBN 0-553-21796-8

Published simultaneously in the United States and Canada

Bantam Books are published by Bantam Books, Inc. Its trademark, consisting of the words "Bantam Books" and the por-
trayal of a rooster, is Registered in U.S. Patent and Trademark
Office and in other countries. Marca Registrada. Bantam
Books, Inc., 666 Fifth Avenue, New York, New York 10103.

PRINTED IN THE UNITED STATES OF AMERICA

O      0 9 8 7 6 5 4 3 2 1

# One

A slow newsday, and still it was chaos in the newsroom of the *Los Angeles Daily*. Adam Mac-Hugh ignored the telephones, the electronic noises from typewriters and computers, the background voices. He was absorbed by the article in his hands.

A memo landed in front of him with a loud slap, and there was Polanski, palms flat on his desk.

"Had a busy morning, MacHugh?" she asked with biting politeness.

He sat back in his wide chair, his elbows on its arms, his fingertips touching. Taking his time, he studied his opponent. Hair the color of wild honey, eyes a rare dark blue, she had beauty. But he'd stopped being fooled by the softness of her looks a long time ago, and right now there wasn't a doubt in his mind. Kate Polanski was spitting mad.

Mac's face became unreadable as he spoke in a low rumble. "Good morning, Kate." He'd been expecting her for over an hour and in just such a mood. This time she wasn't going to get to him.

Kate leaned closer, challenge in her eyes. "Don't play cat and mouse with me, MacHugh."

His arms tensed before he spoke. "Why don't you take it to the source, Polanski?"

Kate heard the edge in his voice. She tilted her

chin up and answered without guile. "I thought I had."

Mac's eyes snapped with annoyance at that. Across the aisle, his friend Rob Dunham grinned and rubbed his hands together. Mac sent him a glare, but it had no visible effect on Rob.

"Was this your idea," Kate continued, looking down at Mac, "or did you just get lucky?" Phones throughout the newsroom were now ringing without answer.

Mac stared back at her, his mouth a hard line. "Cool off, Polanski," he said at last. He could feel his blood pressure rise, but he was trying to stay calm. His brows drew together with the effort.

"Maybe I will. Maybe." She pushed defiantly at a fallen curl and her eyes narrowed. "When you explain this." She pointed to the memo she had thrown on his desk. "This is my story and I don't want or need you on it."

Mac rose in one long, slow motion until he towered over her. "I do not believe," he said through clenched teeth, "that I have the patience to explain anything to you without murdering you, Polanski. So"—he gave her a level look—"why don't you and I go see Joe?" His cool bothered her, he could tell. "He's still in the conference room."

"Fine," Kate said shortly.

"Fine," Mac answered back, and together they marched to the glass door. He noticed that her head scarcely cleared his shoulder.

Once there, Mac reached for the door, meaning to go first, but Kate stepped neatly in front of him. Still in the doorway, she stopped, throwing a "that's one for me" look over her shoulder. Then, leaning his way, she sniffed lightly, glanced uncaringly at his too good-looking face, and smiled.

"Eau de lady-killer, MacHugh?" She thought with

satisfaction that she could almost hear his teeth grinding as she left him there.

The room they entered was surrounded on three sides by glass. One man sat at the long table, papers strewn before him. Kate's stride became easy, though her chin stayed high.

"What is this about, Joe?" she asked, walking the length of the table. Her hands were clenched at her sides as she tried to read Joe's expression. Joe took off the glasses he used for reading and studied Kate and Mac.

Joseph T. Bradley had been editor of the *Los Angeles Daily* for nearly fifteen years. Fifty-six on his next birthday, he was twenty-five pounds overweight, gray-haired, gray-eyed, and had more creases in his face than a ten-year-old baseball glove. He thought himself a tough old bird, but in the newsroom they called him Pappy when he wasn't within hearing distance.

Kate had been with him now for almost a year. Joe didn't think about it often, but he was really very fond of her. When he looked at Kate, he was reminded of demoiselles and gifted painters, pale yellow light and romance. To know her was something else. He liked that.

Her work mixed razor-sharp perception with an overall view, and she had become known for a distinctive writing style and a strange assortment of friends.

Joe pulled a cigarette from the package in his shirt pocket and tamped it on the surface of the table. He saw her eyes flash with a temper usually concealed, and turned his attention to the man behind her.

Like his father, Mac was of the old school. He believed in hard facts, bare-bones insight, and in-depth investigation. He had two reputations, one for being a man of principle, the other as a man women pursued.

Joe looked up at the two reporters and wondered, as he always did, why they hadn't turned out to be friends.

"Sit down, Kate. Mac." He nodded to them both. "I was just going over the proposal on this story." He lit the cigarette casually, watching them through the smoke.

"My story, Joe," Kate said as she took a chair, her gaze steady on her editor.

"Only if I say it is," Joe answered her sternly. He could feel her rebellion, but he sensed Kate had some personal stake in this story and he wasn't pleased. "Mac will be on this with you," he said, wanting no argument. Kate lifted a brow to test him, but he never faltered. "That's just the way it is, Kate."

Finally, she sighed in defeat. "Why MacHugh?" she asked, as if Mac weren't sitting across the table from her.

"Because neither of you are in the middle of important stories. Or am I wrong?" He looked from one set face to the other. "Mac's a good reporter, Kate. Don't let that go to your head," he said in an aside to Mac. "And." He paused again, looking from one to the other. "I want a story."

Kate looked down at the grain of the scarred wooden table before her, then across to her would-be partner. He was watching her with an expression that showed his amusement at the scrutiny.

Mac had struck sparks off Kate from the moment they'd met. She thought he was arrogant. Even his looks annoyed her. He was coolly handsome, with an actor's face and build. Blond too. But it was the way he dealt with women that really got to her.

He smiled, they fell.

The first three months Kate had been on the paper, she had wanted to pound Mac every time he passed her a compliment on a story. He seemed so damned surprised she had done a good job.

And his women . . . Always a beauty, ever a dope.

She might respect his work, but she had very little respect for the man.

"All right," she said, and sighed, giving in because she knew she had no choice. She gave Mac one last look, her only sign of emotion, then turned back to Joe. "But I don't have to like it."

Mac grimaced, nodded at Kate, and wondered what she had against him in the first place. Women usually liked him. Of course, he'd gotten the better assignments in her early months with the paper, and there had been the mix-up on that dam-project story. But he'd always told her when he liked her work, and, he thought with a smile, he liked the look of her.

Not that he was crazy about her. Oh, she was a good and thorough reporter with an interesting style, but there was something about her. Maybe it was the fact that she looked so soft and helpless but wasn't. Or maybe it was just that she couldn't stand him.

She could be pretty rough. He shrugged and smiled wider, wide enough to bother her.

Kate didn't think it nearly as amusing as Mac did. She stood, gave a nod to Joe, a wry look to Mac, then walked to the glass door.

"Well, come on!" she said to her partner, and stalked out. Mac waited until she was through the door before he got to his feet and turned to Joe.

"Outdid yourself this time, Pappy." He shook his head. "I'll get even, you know." But Joe only smiled secretively and went back to his paperwork.

Kate was at her desk when Mac came out, and though her head was turned away as she worked on her computer, he could see the steam was still rising. He might have waited until later to approach her, but he could put up with her bad temper to get a start on this story.

Kate was feeling real panic. MacHugh was going to upset everything, she thought. She saw the dark leather of his shoes when he stopped next to her computer terminal. Her features tightened.

He cleared his throat, waiting. When that didn't help, he leaned lightly on the computer.

"Come on, Polanski. You're going to have to talk to me. I need information. I need to know what you've got and which direction you've already worked. I have a couple of other things in the works, but we might as well give this a go." At least she had stopped using her keyboard, he thought, and looked at his watch. "Look, why don't we go to lunch? Bring your notes and you can fill me in."

Kate looked at him for a few seconds before she pushed the hair out of her eyes one more time. "Give me two minutes to wind this up," she said.

"Good," he answered shortly. He walked back to his own desk some yards away. Rob was there waiting for him, eyes closed, feet up.

Rob and Mac had been college roommates, and their friendship had lasted through football seasons, girls, the death of Mac's brother, first jobs, Rob's marriage and its later breakup. One never let the other get away with a thing. Rob had only been here on the *Daily* for a few months. He'd spent the last two years on a Washington paper. But already he and Mac had slipped back into the old patterns.

"So what did you do to sweet little Katie Polanski?" Rob asked, fast on the attack. Mac pushed his feet off the desk in one swipe and grinned.

"She still turning you down, Robbie?"

"She just can't stand the idea of going out with a friend of yours." Rob laughed and looked up at Mac. "Whatever started this thing anyway? You grab her in the elevator or something?"

Mac straightened a few scattered notes on his desk, got a new pad from the drawer, and shook his head. "Can't figure it out." Then he stood still. "There's only one thing I can think of. You know, when she first started on the paper, she submitted the idea for that dam-safety story. Pappy was on vacation and an assignment editor put me on it. I didn't even know it was hers."

"Bingo," Rob said, getting lazily to his feet. He leaned an elbow on the chest-high partition on one side of Mac's desk. "I believe you got some kind of award for that story?" He raised a sandy brow.

Mac rubbed his chin. "There's only one other possibility," he said with a grin, staring down into a drawer. "Polanski could be after my body."

Kate had walked up behind them just in time to hear the last.

"Ready, big guy?" she asked the back of Mac's neck with grim humor. She then took great pleasure watching Rob's face fold in horror as Mac stiffened. Neither of them moved.

"You take your time," she said sweetly. "I'll just meet you at the elevator." Mac nodded his head way up and way down. When she was gone he sighed heavily.

"I'm dead," he said with his eyes squeezed shut.

"Bingo," Rob said.

Kate and Mac didn't speak as they left the building. She had seen him coming and pressed the elevator button. By the time he reached her she was already inside, holding the doors. In the elevator Mac stared at the panel to his right, down at his shoes, then directly before him.

When the doors opened he waited for Kate to exit first. He didn't see the smile she turned to the wall of the elevator. He reached for the knot of his tie and followed her. Damned thing was too tight, he thought. He was only wearing it because he had to go to court later.

It figures that she would wear pants, he mused, looking at the loose white linen jacket over beige linen trousers moving ahead of him. Yesterday he'd heard her wisecracking with two other reporters about Pappy's latest go-around with the lawyers upstairs. Just one of the guys.

Kate slid the sleeves of her jacket up to her elbows and tried to resign herself to the idea that she and Mac were a team. She'd watched him work on a story before. He had good instincts. Of course, that could pose another problem. She didn't want anyone questioning her interest in this story, or in a man named Ferranti.

"Mario's?" she asked over one shoulder. He grunted in response. She walked on, still ahead, and he made no effort to catch up.

Mario's was a little Italian restaurant around the corner from the paper. Kate saw the pink neon sign, dull now against the midday sun. With one hand on the carved door, she waited for Mac. At his approach she entered and held the door. There, for the first time, she realized how tall Mac was, how broad his chest. She assumed he passed so close to her so that she would be intimidated.

She wasn't.

Meanwhile Mario of Mario's was peeking through the diamond-shaped window of the kitchen door, as he did from time to time to make sure all was well. When he saw Kate the door flew open with a bang of enthusiasm.

"Katerina!" he bellowed. *"Che bella!"* He raised his arms high. *"Va bene, cara mia?"* Kate looked self-consciously at Mac, who mouthed "Katerina?" before she moved in for the offered hug.

"Mario." She smiled warmly and returned his two-cheek kiss. *"Va bene, Mario. Come stai?"* He answered in a spate of Italian only a native would comprehend. "Mario," she said, pulling herself from his arms, "this is Adam MacHugh from the paper."

"But yes, Katerina," Mario said, beaming. "I know Mac for a long time." He held out a beefy hand. "How you been, my friend?" Turning to Kate, Mario added, "We have done many favors for each other, yes, Mac?" which earned him a wary look from Kate that Mac didn't understand. Suddenly, Mario stage-whispered to Kate, "He likes pesto, cara. I give you my recipe!" And Mac got to see little Katie Polanski blush rose-red as she let loose in Italian.

And that was only the first surprise. Her voice was rich, full with the melodies of the language, as she scolded in outrage. Her face, too, was alive with emotion that highlighted her beautiful high cheekbones, shining eyes, and blurred mobile mouth.

All innocence, Mario defended himself, and a tiny laugh wrinkled Kate's nose as she hid behind one hand. Mac could hardly believe his eyes. There was such warmth, such sweetness about the woman before him. She was so completely at odds with the tough professional, which was all Mac had ever been allowed to see. At last Kate shook her head, and finished in English.

"And Mama! I think she would have something to say about the way you disgrace me!"

*"Ecco!"* Mario bent his head in mock remorse,

well aware of his role in the game they played. Still contrite, he gestured to a booth, then said something else very quickly in Italian to Kate before heading to the kitchen.

Kate looked at Mac. The color remained in her face as she said, "I'm sorry. He's making fettucini Alfredo for us." She grimaced, slightly, drawing Mac's gaze to the softness of her mouth. "He thinks I'm too skinny."

"No." Mac smiled slowly, and said without emphasis, "Not skinny."

Her tone became casual. "At least there'll be antipasto first." She moved to the booth to get away from the heat in Mac's eyes as much as to have something to do. Again he followed.

When they were settled Mac let his glance drift over her fair skin, her honey-colored hair. "Um," he began, "you're name *is* Polanski, isn't it, Katerina?" He tried not to smile, she tried not to smile, and Kate had never liked him so well. In fact, she was beginning to like him entirely too much. That little-boy look he had was working on her.

"My mother's Italian," she said shortly, and suddenly Mac found himself out in the cold again.

He didn't like the feeling. He had just gotten a taste of what he suspected was the real Kate. He was becoming very interested. "How do you know Mario," he asked, "through family or the paper?"

He was trying to regain lost ground and she knew it. But her smile was not for him.

"Oh, Mario's been in love with my mother for years." Then Kate leaned across the table. "He's making the fettucini himself, MacHugh, so be a good guy." She whispered as if she didn't expect it.

Mac placed his elbows on the table. When he lifted his chin she saw the indentation in the middle of it. Finally he asked, "Just what is it you have against me, Polanski?"

The question startled her, and she hoped she hid it well. "Let's stick to the story, Mac." She looked up as the waiter rescued her with coffee for them both. "If you'd prefer something else . . . ?" she asked politely.

"No," Mac said, annoyed that she had dodged his question. "Mario knows what I want." Then he blanched at his own words. He hadn't meant a thing by them, but he was certain she would think he did. The coffee he gulped burned his mouth, but he swallowed bravely. Another save by the waiter, this time with antipasto. By the time the man left Mac had decided there was only one safe subject. Kate must have agreed, because she ignored the food long enough to rummage in her briefcase for her notepad and a pencil. With them beside her plate, she took up her fork.

"So," she said between bites, her voice all business once more, "how much did Joe tell you?"

"Only enough to tease me," Mac answered dryly. Kate knew Pappy's technique and couldn't help a bit of a smile.

"Then I'll start at the beginning." She waited only for his nod. "The L.A. County Museum is preparing for an exhibit of ancient Chinese art to open on the twenty-fifth of this month. There are pieces in this exhibit that have never before been allowed to leave China. But, due to poor communications about schedule changes, the exhibit arrived early."

"Is that a problem?"

"Yes and no. Have you ever heard of Riccardo Ferranti?"

Mac searched his mind for the familiar name, but before he could connect Kate pulled a photograph from her briefcase and handed it to him. As Mac

studied the man's face—he was distinguished looking, perhaps fifty-five—Kate continued.

"Ferranti was a notorious art thief in Europe in
the late forties, early fifties. Monaco, the Riviera,
London, Rome. After he retired he began security
consulting with museums and private collectors,
insurance companies." Kate looked up from her
notes and put down the pencil. "His firm was
contracted by the museum to monitor this exhibit. When the foul-up occurred two days ago,
the independent Mr. Ferranti checked out of his
hotel and absconded with the exhibit. For *safe-
keeping*, he said." Kate looked up, her eyes twin-
kling. "Of course, the lines have become a little
hot between cultural affairs offices, hotter still
when China asked for Ferranti's dossier." She
glanced back down at her notes. "However, Ferranti
has a contract with the museum that gives him
complete autonomy. He says he intends to keep
the whereabouts of the exhibit a secret until a few
days before the twenty-fifth . . . when he will
deliver."

Kate stopped toying with her fork and looked
directly at the man across from her. "That much
of the story will be in the evening edition. This
won't." She leaned forward, lowering her voice.
"Ferranti seems to be playing hide-and-seek with
the authorities. No one trusts him, but no one's
got anything on him; he hasn't made one illegal
move. I saw him last night, at a party." She gave a
quick laugh. "With a police detective, no less."

She was interrupted by the appearance of Mario, a waiter at each elbow. *"Andiamo! Andiamo!"*
Mario, pleased with himself, grandly directed
the exchange of plates with a two-foot pepper-
mill. When he was finished he announced, "This
you will like!" and made a grand turn before
his exit. Kate kept her eyes down to hide her

laughter. Mac made an odd noise deep in his throat.

Into the air Kate whispered softly, "This is Italian matchmaking!" But she wouldn't look at Mac.

They ate for a few minutes in silence. Mac spoke first, laying down his fork. "What were you doing there?" he asked casually. "At the party."

"I had heard Ferranti was invited." She tried to be equally casual.

He made a small sound of acknowledgment, and picked up his cup. Mac had been a reporter for a long time. He could usually tell when a subject was hiding something, and Kate Polanski had just made herself a subject. He looked up from his coffee to ask another question. "You got a friend at an embassy, or something?"

"Look, Mac, I think there are a couple of things we need to discuss before we start working together." He waited. "I don't answer to you. I don't reveal my methods or my sources unless absolutely necessary. By that I mean unless it's to my editor, a grand jury, or you—if you don't believe me. But if I guarantee confidentiality, I'll dump a story before I'll reveal the source." She placed her napkin carefully on the table near her fork. "Joe and I have an understanding. If possible, we accommodate each other. We compromise, but not with principles." She rested her folded arms on the edge of the table, looked down, then back up at Mac. "I think you're a first-rate, ethical reporter, Mac. But I'm used to working alone; trust doesn't come easily for me." There, she thought, that sounded all right, didn't it?

Mac was impressed. Kate was pretty good at confusing the issue, but he believed the game lay in the subtext. "So, don't ask a direct question unless it's essential?"

She had underestimated him, Kate thought. He

was telling her he didn't trust her either. "I know a few people, Mac, just like you do. Okay?"

"Okay," he said simply, smiling in a way she found she liked. And for a moment they looked at each other, no longer enemies.

"So . . ." he said slowly, "what do you say we do the preliminary work apart, try to locate Ferranti, compare notes every night or if something special comes up."

Kate nodded, picking up her coffee cup.

"Oh, and Katerina . . ." he said lightly, tearing off a piece of bread.

Here it comes, she thought, the "little woman" routine. He was going to tell her how dangerous this was and how he'd do his best to protect them both.

But Mac only looked her over dispassionately and lifted the bread to his mouth.

"You've got fettucini Alfredo on your chin," he said.

# Two

This kind of excitement was addicting, Kate thought. It created a special fever, an awareness of life. It was one reason she stayed in a profession that could be hard and cold and full of risk. It was one reason she loved that profession.

The night was closet-dark, with hardly a star in the sky. But then she'd never been afraid of the dark. And . . . there was a feeling in the air here, a heaviness that said something was about to happen.

Whatever it was, Kate Polanski had no intention of missing it.

The call had come late tonight, but more than one story had fallen her way because of a phone call in the middle of the night. She had asked a fellow reporter, one who habitually haunted the Beverly Hills police station, to let her know if Detective Jarré was overheard on the phone with anyone with an Italian name.

Luck had played a hand, and here she was, hiding against the wall of an ancient warehouse near Santa Monica in Beverly Hills, waiting. She checked her watch, then her camera and tape recorder. After a last look over the grounds she knelt before the small side door and pulled a pencil flashlight and soft leather case from a back pocket.

Her uncle Tony had given her the locksmith's kit on her fourteenth birthday. She remembered the afternoons she had spent in his shop, learning to use it. Within a month she had known more about locks than many dedicated thieves.

The warehouse had a double-key lock that took less than a minute. Genes, Kate thought with a half-smile as she heard the click. She packed the tools away and opened the door with professional quiet.

She blinked into the darkness, scanning the area, trying to feel for another presence or for boxes in storage.

Nothing.

Swinging the beam of her flashlight, she saw that the warehouse was truly empty, nothing but dirt on the floor and an old worktable at one end. No place to hide.

Retracing her steps, she slid out through the door and pressed against the wall beside it, closing the door until she could see only a sliver of black. Then she settled back to wait.

Mac would be sorry—maybe even mad—to have missed this, she thought, but she had called him, both at home and at the paper. It was just her good fortune not to have found him.

In the four days they had been working on this story, they had spent very little time together. Most of their inquiries had been made by phone, and so far they had found out nothing concrete. Ferranti had temporarily disappeared. Tonight's call was the first bit of action.

She readjusted her black cap, tucking in a wisp of hair and pulling the bill low over her eyes. Then she heard a sound.

It was the scrape of a metal door on concrete,

and her heart counted in half seconds. She heard the scuffle of hard-soled shoes, then the fragile light of a naked bulb threw shadows. Ignoring the pounding of her heart, she moved toward the door.

Suddenly, an arm clamped around her waist. The weight of it carried her to the bushes nearby and shoved her to the ground. The man stayed in a crouch beside her, his arm heavy on her back.

Kate's throat had closed in terror, her body tensed for a struggle, when she took in a breath . . . and relaxed. She recognized the scent. Of course, she'd never been quite this close to him before. She sniffed and turned her face to his with a pained, significant expression. He merely looked annoyed and checked the area for signs of movement. .

"So," she said in a low voice, "you're following me, Mac?"

His mouth was tight as he looked down at her again, then away. "Nice message you left me, partner. 'There's a meeting at a warehouse on Little Santa Monica. I'll get back to you.' " His imitation of her voice was terrible. The arm that surrounded her began to feel like steel, and Kate could see Mac's perfect white teeth clenched together. "Do you know how many warehouses there are on this block alone?" he whispered furiously.

She shook her head no.

"The only reason I found you at all," he went on, "is because I saw your car parked down the street." He dragged in a breath. "Dammit, Polanski! You could be dead by now!"

At that, a small sound of amusement escaped her. "Really, Mac, this is about art, not murder."

He rolled his eyes up. "Of all the naive— We're not talking five-and-dime here, Polanski, we're talking about millions of dollars! And the guy who just went into your warehouse is a cop with a shoulder holster who has no idea you're an idiot reporter who just wants to tag along to see if anything happens!"

"They're here?" Kate struggled out from under him, suddenly remembering that she wanted to be inside that warehouse by now. "Mac." She squirmed. "Let me . . . up!" She twisted around to give him a dirty look and caught just a glimpse of his eyes before he flattened her with his own body. Her chin slapped the ground and her teeth went into her lower lip. The cap fell over her eyes and she tasted blood. The worst was that she couldn't move. He weighed a ton.

"Dammit, MacHugh!" she complained into the grass. She dragged her elbows in for leverage as she managed to push back her cap with one finger. "I know your mating technique is legendary"— an elbow was sliding and she fell flat on the ground again—"but couldn't you let just one get away?"

There was a grunt in response, but he only lifted his head to survey the area and the situation. "Ferranti," he said at last. Kate's head came up at that, the tension back in her body.

"Mac, you're breaking my ribs." She made another attempt to move before finally using a sharp elbow in his side. He cursed in a low voice, but this time he moved off her, rubbing his stomach as he pulled her to a sitting position. He stayed on one knee while Kate felt around for her camera.

"Too bad we don't work together more often," she muttered, not in the least grateful for the protection of that hard body.

"He's gone in," Mac said, and finally glanced down at her. "You're bleeding." His mouth softened in surprise and he touched a finger to her lip.

"How much do you weigh?" she asked as she touched the cut herself and winced.

"Mm, sorry," he said, and wiped the blood from her chin with his thumb. His touch was gentle.

Their eyes met, then they looked away.

"Look, Mac," Kate said. "I want to go in there . . . and I want you to stay outside." She held up a hand. "I know, you want to go, but I've been in there. There's no place to hide. You're too big." She looked at him, trying to convince him. "You can stay right outside the door. You can be the cavalry if you have to—but I want to go in alone. I didn't have to call you, you know." She stared into his eyes with everything she felt. "Mac?"

He took his time, holding off his instinctive refusal. Without really understanding why, he changed his mind. "Okay," he said reluctantly, "but don't get caught."

She smiled. "That," she said gently, "is something you don't have to worry about."

There was such sweetness in the look she gave him, and he felt a kind of camaraderie he had never known with a woman before. Mac suddenly realized that he liked this girl-woman with her bad manners and defiance and romantic beauty.

"Let's go," he said quickly, before he gave himself time to think about what he was agreeing to do. Kate scrambled after him. When they were beside the warehouse's back door she sent him one last look, and he put his palm to her cheek. "Take care," he said.

She thought his words were antiquated and beautiful. She gave a small nod and slipped through the door.

From far away, almost the entire length of the warehouse, she could see the two men. One of them moved and the light fell on his face. Kate recognized him immediately. His build was lean, muscular—interesting in a man of his years. He had to be in his early fifties. The gray hair was streaked with white, and he had the sculpted beard of the poet-pirate. An attractive man, she mused, forcing an objective distance to her thoughts, definitely European. Her attention turned to the man beside him, and she inched closer.

The second man was the detective she had seen before, at the party she had attended. His name was Jarré. Younger than Ferranti, he didn't look like a cop. He was tall, well dressed, with ascetic features and feline stance.

Her hand moved to her camera. The film was infrared. Kate knew if she were to get a shot, it would have to be from this distance or the click of the shutter might betray her. She took four quick ones in succession and pushed the camera under the sweater she wore, tucking it in at her waist.

Then, without a sound of warning, a third man entered the small sphere of light. The detective made motions of introductions between the new man and Ferranti. They spoke in quiet tones. Kate would have to move closer if she wanted to hear them.

Just for a second, she glanced back over her shoulder to where she knew Mac waited for her. Then she took a deep, silent breath and turned back to the light. She could feel her heart pounding as she concentrated on moving toward it. Her sneaker scraped over a nail with a noise she thought deafening, and adrenaline shot through her in panic.

But they didn't stop, didn't turn. She forced her breathing to slow before going farther. She couldn't afford mistakes.

"This will be ideal for my purposes," she heard Ferranti say. He spoke in a melodic voice, the accent noticeable.

"Good," the third man said and smiled. He

was dressed casually but expensively, a fat cat—late fifties, obviously from Beverly Hills.

"When will it be available for me?" Ferranti asked, gazing around the warehouse. "I'd like to have my security people take a look at it."

"I can give you the keys now," came the answer.

"Excellent," said Ferranti, and glanced again into the darkness around him. Kate held her breath; she was too close. But the three men began to move casually toward the far door, speaking in quiet tones. The detective went out first, "Beverly Hills" flicked the light switch and followed him, then waited in the doorway for his new client. But Riccardo Ferranti paused in the darkness, an alertness in his stance, only his shape distinguishable in silhouette.

Instinct, Kate thought with a thrill of fear and exhilaration. She almost wanted to be caught, just to see what he would do. But he turned, murmuring something to the other men, and the door closed behind him with a metallic bang.

Kate hurried to the back door, but just as she pushed from the inside, Mac pulled, and she landed at his feet.

"They've gone," he said, then leaned down. "Kate? You're all right aren't you?"

"Mmmm," she answered dryly. "Just feeling a bit fragile."

He reached down a hand to her. "Give me a ride?" he asked as he pulled her up too quickly. She rammed into him. "Sorry," he said under his breath. Kate closed her eyes and tried not to imagine another hour's worth of bruises.

"Where's your car?" she asked automatically as she started to walk.

"The shop."

She halted in midstep. "You took a cab here?" she asked accusingly. She looked him up and down, set the lock of the warehouse door, then stalked toward her car mumbling, "How inconspicuous . . . taking a cab to a deserted warehouse." Mac wore a small grin that said he enjoyed getting a rise out of her.

Once in the car Kate watched him settle himself, and, hand on the gearshift, she asked, "Home or the paper?"

"Home," he said, giving her the address near Griffith Park. "So," he continued, turning in his seat to face her. She was pulling her camera from beneath her sweater and Mac found himself wanting more than the glimpse of pale skin he was given. "What happened?"

Kate kept her attention on the rearview mirror as she began to maneuver out of her hiding place behind a truck. "Don't tell me you weren't watching, MacHugh, because you don't have a chance of making me believe it."

He smiled in answer. "No, I mean what did they say, what was the deal they made?"

She shook her head. "It sounded like Ferranti had Jarré—the cop—introduce him to the man who owned the warehouse. They made a deal for Ferranti to use it." There was a car coming from behind her. She would wait for it to pass before she turned on her own headlights. "I'll check ownership on Monday," she finished, hoping Mac wouldn't ask any more questions.

He was still watching her face. "And . . ." he said expectantly.

"And what?" She chanced a look his way.

"I have a *feeling*"—he made the word sound like ESP—"that there is something you're not telling me."

Kate wasn't going to argue with him. She

reached for the radio and his hand met hers on the dial. His hand was wide and strong, the texture of his skin rough . . . disturbing.

"Kate," he said quietly. She snatched her hand away.

"I'm only mad at myself for finding Ferranti and not getting any information," she said in a rush.

He was still watching her. "Why the camera?"

She shrugged.

As the dark Mercedes finally, moved by them, she stiffened. "Mac, that's him—there he goes!"

"Who?" Mac wondered how she could see inside the car's tinted windows.

"Ferranti. It's Ferranti! I'm going to follow him!" And she was after him.

Mac pressed one hand against the dash. "Was there anyone else in the car?" he asked.

"I don't know. At least a driver. Ferranti's in the backseat." Kate concentrated on the Mercedes's taillights as she made a U-turn around the high hedge that separated Little Santa Monica's warehouses from the four busy lanes of Santa Monica that ran the length of Beverly Hills. There was traffic, too much traffic.

The Mercedes pulled into the left lane and Kate followed, then cursed softly when the dark car switched lanes.

"Ask this woman if she'll let us over," Kate said, referring to the car on their right. Mac stuck his head out the window and gestured with a smile. The move was made with track speed, and Mac was left holding the base of the window with both hands. The look he turned to Kate was menacing.

"Finally, a use for all that irresistible charm," she muttered. He ignored the comment. Ferranti was two cars ahead, and moving back into the left lane.

"He's got his signal on," Mac said. "He's going to make this right."

"From that lane?" Kate was outraged. She took the corner after him, tires squealing, and suddenly there were three dark Mercedeses, two in the same lane. Her brows lifted in comical surprise and Mac burst into unrestrained laughter.

"Let's get to work," Kate said, grinning a small unwilling grin. "You remember anything about his plates?"

"Just California." Mac waited until her face fell. "But I do remember a nick in the glass of his left taillight."

"Why, Mac . . ." She looked at him with new respect. "You're beginning to pay your way."

"Oh, I have a few talents," he teased.

"Really?" she said, her tone dry. "There's one that hasn't worn down with use?"

He cleared his throat.

"Benedict Canyon," he announced a few minutes later, as the road wound into the hills. Kate changed lanes again and Mac grabbed for the doorstrap. "Do you think he's got a place up here? Or maybe he's going to the valley."

"We'll find out." Kate's chin lifted. "Look, he's turning again."

Her Volkswagen had no trouble with the steep curve, but the way was narrow, and Kate had to keep her attention on the road. "See anything?"

"Not yet," Mac was leaning forward, watching both sides of the road for a parked Mercedes. There was no sign of it on the street ahead. "Wait, look up there. Slow down, Kate. I think that's it." A modern, wide-windowed house stood facing the view from the ridge. The car in the drive was definitely the one they'd been following. Kate looked for a place without a curb where she could pull over and be out of the road. Fifteen yards after the house, she stopped the car abruptly.

"You drive like a maniac," Mac said.

"I know," she said with great satisfaction.

"Cops and robbers. Now what?" he whispered.

Kate's eyes were wide and sparkling in the dark, her smile cockeyed because of the tender lip. "I think this is where we improvise." She sent him a sidelong glance. "Any ideas?"

"Well." He was watching lights come on in the house, room by room. "We could go over what we've got." Kate said nothing.

"I'm wondering about that meeting," he went on, tapping one finger on his bent knee. "How did you know about it. One of those mysterious sources of yours?"

She nodded. "A friend at the Beverly Hills station."

"He give you any details?"

"No." She looked away, uncomfortable. "I was asleep when he called," she muttered. Mac didn't comment, but he was pleased to have caught her for once without her cool, professional shell. "Did you get anything today?" she asked, willing the heat from her cheeks.

He leaned back in the small seat. "Actually, I did find out that Ferranti has accepted invitations to several functions in Beverly Hills. I think your idea of sticking close to Ferranti is the best bet we've got."

"What do you think about Jarré? Do you think he knows where it is?"

"You think he does?"

"They're old friends. Jarré knew Ferranti in Paris." She rubbed her chin. "But I don't believe our man trusts anyone."

Mac shook his head. "We don't really have anything concrete, we don't even know who wants him." He ran a hand through his hair, then looked at Kate closely. "You wouldn't be holding out on me, would you, Polanski?"

She just stared back at him, her expression cold. "Well," she said at last, glancing up at the house, "he doesn't seem to be going anywhere tonight. And now we know his home base. We might as well go." She started the car. "What time is it?"

"Twelve-fifteen." Mac was trying to read her face, but he wasn't getting anywhere. With a sigh he gave the house one last glance, and froze. "Kate, turn off the motor!"

She acted first, asked second. "What—"

"Ferranti's on the terrace. He's seen us." Kate turned her head to Mac, slowly, carefully. She saw the outline of a man. He was definitely looking their way. She leaned closer to Mac, laying her cheek against his, staring out the back window.

"Should I consider this a pass?" he asked eagerly, and Kate could feel his smile as his beard scraped her cheek. "Or are we going to neck in the line of duty?"

"Put your arm around me, you tired Casanova, and save the lines for those subintellects you frequent," Kate whispered lovingly into his ear. "We have to stay here until he loses interest. But if you kiss me, you'll be sore for a week."

He was still smiling, she could feel it. Then his head bent to the warm place where her neck joined her shoulder. He spoke against her skin. "You smell sweet." Her chin lifted as she tried to move away, but now his arms came around her, pulling her over the emergency brake and partway across the space between them.

"Will you—" she started furiously, pushing at his shoulders. He drew her hard to him. Her face pressed against his shoulder where her hand had been. She could feel her heart beat crazily against his, and it annoyed her that hers pounded while his stayed steady.

"Now, now, Polanski," he said into her hair. "Just business." She "hmffed" once and relaxed in his arms, waiting. That was when she became aware that her sweater had ridden up above her waist and one of his hands lay on her skin. She was twisted at an odd angle too. "This is extremely uncomfortable," she told his shoulder, and the words had hardly left her mouth when he was hauling her again, this time into his lap.

"Dammit, MacHugh, you are the most—"

"Now you'll have to kiss me," he said, smiling into her face just above his. "He can see us better like this." And when Kate looked back at the house to see if what he said was true, Mac took advantage of her inattention and kissed her.

His lips were warm and soft on hers, gentle with a persuasion she did not expect. When they left hers, it was only to brush a corner of her mouth. Her mouth opened, in surprise, she thought, and his tongue touched the small cut her teeth had made before he kissed that too.

"No," she said in reflex, and wondered why it sounded so weak.

Maybe he didn't hear her, she mused, as he kissed her again, and his searching tongue moved over the cut and into her mouth. The angle of the kiss changed again and again, its sweetness stabbing at her. Strong and quick was the beat of his heart now, and Kate shivered as she said no once more into his mouth. He refused to listen as he deepened the kiss. She thought she wouldn't want it to stop in a few more seconds. And then he pulled away, with one last gentle touch of his lips to hers. He looked out the window and spoke, his voice nearly even.

"He's gone now."

Kate scrambled awkwardly over to the driver's seat. Staring straight ahead into the black of night, she moved jerkily to start the car as she tried to erase the feel of him from her senses. She turned on the lights, looked up and down the length of the street, and put the car into gear.

Neither knew what to say, so for twenty minutes neither spoke.

"I'll see what I can find out tomorrow," Kate finally said, turning the corner onto Mac's street. "I know a bartender at a place near the precinct station. I think Jarré goes there."

She stopped the car when Mac said, "This one on the left," then turned sideways, waiting for him to get out. Eye to eye, it was a standoff.

He needed a shave, she thought, and his hair curled over the collar of his denim shirt. He was rude, arrogant, overbearing, chauvinistic, a womanizer, and too damned good-looking. Worse, he affected her.

Mac had been studying her in return. Strange, he thought. He'd protected her by instinct, and had been startled when he had felt the softness of her body under him. Looking at her now, at the shine of her golden hair under the cap, her full mouth and stubborn chin, the fine straight nose and dark blue eyes, he felt a sudden rush of heat. Ridiculous, he told himself. This was business, and there was something she wasn't telling him. He knew it every time he looked at her.

"If you come in a minute, I'll give you a cold pack for that lip," he offered, thinking it was a fair ploy. She didn't go for it.

"Thanks, Mac," she said in refusal, and he could see that she was trying to hold a smile. It kept slipping. "I think I'll just go home and see if I can get this lovely scent out of my clothes." She bent her head in innocence and sent him an upward glance. "But you can get a fresh start on me tomorrow."

He set his jaw, climbed out of the car, and walked around to her open window. "You know, Polanski," he said mildly, "you're not half as tough as you think you are."

"Aah," she answered thoughtfully, revving the engine before smiling brightly. "But how"—she put the car into first—"will you ever prove it?" And with that, she pressed her foot on the gas, leaving Mac in the street looking after her.

Mac turned and started up the walk, one hand digging in his pocket for keys. Just for a second he saw Kate Polanski again as she had looked playing "got you last" in the street.

He nearly smiled.

# *Three*

It was four in the morning. Kate was lying in bed, the expression in her eyes deep and vulnerable as she stared at the shadow patterns on the ceiling.

"Ferranti." She whispered the name aloud to those shadows. It had the sound of Venetian princes, Roman nobility. With a sad smile for the whimsy, she wondered what she would have done if she had been caught by Ferranti in that warehouse. The smile deepened as she decided John Wayne MacHugh would probably have come leaping to the rescue.

MacHugh.

She'd resented him a long time, disliked him heartily. But the strangest thing had begun to happen. She was enjoying his company. There was a certain electricity in it. And that kiss . . . Closing her eyes, she remembered its sweetness.

In fact, if it had gone on any longer, she might very well have made a complete fool of herself. Another conquest for MacHugh . . . Horrible thought.

Well, tomorrow there was Sunday dinner at the big house. For just a moment she contemplated skipping Mama's Sunday dinner, but then she smiled and shook her head. The last time she had failed to appear, her uncle had sent two cousins to her house to find out what had happened to her. When they had discovered she wasn't home, they had knocked on every door in the neighborhood trying to find out where she was.

Her cousin Pietro was a six-feet-seven professional basketball player, and Angelo a six-two weight-lifting actor. They had made quite an impression on Kate's neighbors.

The time before that, Uncle Tony had camped on her doorstep until she had returned home. Then for forty long minutes he had scolded her with phrases like "break your mother's heart," "family is everything," and "why won't you go out with that nice young friend of Angelo's?" Now she tried to get to her mother's Sunday dinner whether she was on a story or not. It paid.

She wondered fleetingly what her family would make of MacHugh, then laughed as she imagined Mama pumping him full of lasagna while Uncle Tony asked about his future prospects. Pietro and Angelo would glower across the table while their wives, Tina and Marianna, flirted with Mac. Hmm, that could be good.

But Kate never brought men home for Sunday dinner, and even her loving, pushy family had stopped suggesting it. Kate fell asleep thinking that she must remember to bring Mama some fresh basil from the yard and that the fruit trees needed pruning.

She was having a dream, full of mists and colors. Morning light edged the blinds that fought to keep it from the room, but in the dream there was no time, only color and feeling.

Her head moved on the pillow in unconscious imitation of herself in the dream and one hand reached out into the air. Her heartbeat quickened in both the real and unreal before her eyes suddenly opened wide and she sat up, throwing the covers from her.

A dream . . . only a dream.

Dragging air into her lungs, she slid her legs over the side of the bed. The floor was cool beneath her feet. Her hands trembled as they covered her eyes.

Her heart still defied her as she stumbled to the window and opened the narrow blinds, filling the room with bright streams of light.

She'd always had vivid, realistic dreams, sometimes happy, sometimes frightening. But to have a dream like that . . . about a man like him . . .

Kate took a deep breath and let it out slowly, then took another, and another. She ran her tongue over her still swollen lip and pulled the thin lace gown up and over her head. She'd shower, then she'd make a few phone calls. She'd drop by that precinct bar after the brunch hour. There was no way she was going to face Mac again without information. She frowned, walking to the bathroom. No. The only one she had to answer to was herself.

One step farther and there came the shrill ring of the telephone.

"Hello?" Her voice was husky with lack of sleep.

"Polanski?" Mac said hoarsely. The sound of her voice had just given him a vision of her . . . in bed.

"Yes, Mac." She knew she didn't sound glad to hear from him. She wasn't. She cradled the phone against her shoulder and crossed her arms over her bare breasts.

Her tone didn't even slow him down. "I thought I'd go with you to check out that bartender today."

Her eyes narrowed. "What's up? Don't you trust me, Mac?"

"Oh, come on, Kate." He didn't bother to hide his impatience. "We're on this together, remember?" Why had he expected this to be easy? he wondered. There was only silence on the other end before he finally heard her sigh.

"Okay. But not till three o'clock. I'll meet you where he works."

"What's the matter with now?" It came out more harshly than he had intended. "I'll even buy you breakfast," he said, trying to soften his tone.

Why today? Kate thought miserably, gazing at the ceiling. "Look, I have an appointment first, Mac." Great. He'd think she was working on the story without him. "And they get a brunch crowd on Sundays," she added hastily.

"An appointment," he repeated with no expression.

"I can't be free until after three o'clock."

"No way, Kate."

"What?"

"I said no way. It's obvious you're trying to work on this on your own, and it's more than obvious you're hiding something." He let that sink in. "So, where you go, I go."

This was too good to be true, Kate thought with a silly smile. "Sorry, Mac, you're not invited." She didn't want him to back out now.

"I'm coming," he said definitely, belligerently. "I'll be at your place in five minutes."

"Make it half an hour, I just got up," she said, acting reluctant.

"So you can leave me a note on the front door?" He was a cynic, she thought. "Five minutes . . . I've got the address." He hung up.

Kate was in and out of the shower in those five minutes, but Mac was already leaning on the bell. She came to the door in a white terry robe with a towel wrapped around her head, and met him with a grin.

"You really are a pain, MacHugh," she said, a hand on one hip. He looked surprised by her good mood.

"You got coffee?" he asked, stepping past her.

"Yes." Her gaze followed him into her living room before she closed the door. She tried hard not to be entertained. "You can make it. Kitchen's that way." She pointed to her right, turned to the bedroom, and left him there.

Kate, you're scaring yourself, she said silently to her reflection in the bedroom mirror. What's going on all of a sudden that you notice this man and his hazel eyes and wonder why he isn't wearing cologne . . . for you? She had even found her gaze running down his lean body. He was wearing Sunday casual, white pants and a pale khaki sweater. Again she had to wonder why she noticed. She never had before.

Bending at the waist, she unwrapped the towel from her head so that she could avoid seeing her expression in the mirror. She had to stop herself, too, from thinking about what he might look like without those clothes. Damn. What was happening to her? She wanted her simple, perfect dislike of the man to come back. It would. She was sure of it. All she had to do, she thought with a laugh, was to let him be himself.

Giving her hair a last rub, she threw her head up and found Adam MacHugh standing in the doorway of her bedroom. Strange, the things she became aware of in those few seconds. She knew that her robe had loosened and fallen over one shoulder, that her tangled hair was heavy and cold on her shoulders. And she knew that she had never seen an expression like this on his face before. He looked almost bewildered.

His mouth opened. "How do you take your . . . coffee?" he asked in a voice neither of them recognized.

"Just milk," she said, and tightened the sash of her robe. She had forgotten to adjust it at the shoulder and now it slipped, showing the top of one breast and too much cleavage.

He stared, and she blushed and turned away to pull the robe back into place.

When she looked again at the doorway, he was gone. Her hand went to her hair in an unconscious gesture, then fell to the sash at her waist.


They called it the big house because it sprawled out over three clumsy stories and because it remained the place the Sanducci family gathered for holidays, weddings, and Sunday afternoon dinners.

Turning into the drive, Kate checked the curtained windows. One face peered out from the sea of living room curtains before a corner was dropped with guilty haste. That would be Uncle Tony, Kate thought laughingly. The man had no shame.

"Your appointment is here?" Mac asked Kate. She had driven them both in her car. She looked like the cat that got the cream as she climbed out of the car, and Mac followed suit with a crease between his brows.

What was she dragging him into?

The wooden front steps sounded under their feet, and Kate pushed open the heavy door without ceremony. Mac was just behind her, still cautious.

The things he noticed first had nothing to do with furnishings or design. He noticed sounds and smells. Opera was being played somewhere in the depths of the great house; a football game was on television. The scents in the air were fresh bread, garlic—lots of garlic—tomato sauce, and baking cheese. Mac wished they had stopped for that breakfast.

Just then he bumped into Kate as she stopped too abruptly to let a small dark-haired boy with black eyes and long lashes go running across her path. He was chasing a kitten much faster than he.

"Hey, Mike," Kate said, her voice sweet as she viewed the chase.

"Hi, Aunt Kate," the boy yelled back, never breaking concentration. Mac looked beyond, into the living room where three men sat on the edge of their seats, elbows on their knees, staring at a television. Kate went on ahead, letting Mac trail behind her.

"Hi," she said to the three profiles.

"Hi," they said in random order, without turning. "How you doin', Kate?" one of them asked. She smiled at Mac but didn't bother to answer. Reaching a hand behind her, she pulled on his arm until he was standing beside her.

"Mac," she said with a hint of amusement, "I'd like you to meet Anthony Sanducci, my uncle, and my cousins, Pietro and Angelo." Her will forced them to look her way. "This is Adam MacHugh." Only the older man raised a brow. The other two men just glanced at him with seeming indifference and nodded.

Mac thought the uncle looked like an aging construction worker; big, barrel-chested. His sons were both handsome.

"How do you do, Mr. MacHugh," her uncle said finally in a grim voice. There was a definite old-world accent.

"Nice to meet you," Mac said, feeling something more than uncomfortable.

"Mac works on the paper, Uncle Tony," Kate said.

"Yes," Tony said deliberately. "The dam-project story." His thick black brows rose, then fell. "I remember."

Mac cleared his throat and shifted his feet, delighting Kate. The cousins kept their attention on the game. "Well," Kate said briskly, "I want to take him in to meet Mama and the girls." Tony made a rude noise and turned back to the television. Kate pulled Mac again by the arm. He felt three pairs of eyes on his back as they left.

They walked through the dining room and the sound of classical music grew louder. Kate hummed along until she pushed through the kitchen door. Mac was still hanging back, so she hooked her arm through his and pulled harder. She wouldn't look at him.

Inside, three more pairs of eyes focused on him.

"Hi," Kate said once more as they stood in the doorway.

Mac didn't know what to say.

"I've brought a guest." Kate's smile was pure mischief. "This is Adam MacHugh."

Mac could feel the surprise. For a few seconds no one moved. The opera seemed to become louder, then a woman left the sink to come forward. She had Kate's hair, streaked with lighter blond, but her age showed only in and around her dark blue eyes. She was small-boned, small-figured. Slowly, she walked up to Mac and tilted her head back, looking far up into his eyes. She reached out a hand for his and smiled at him. It was a lovely smile—Kate's. When she spoke, it was with the accent he had come to expect in this house.

"I am Gianetta Polanski. You must call me Gina, and"—her eyes sparkled—"I am happy you have come to share our dinner."

Mac sent Kate a quick glance that was half acknowledgment of the points she had made with this trick, and half the uncertain boy. "I hope *we*"—he refused to take all the blame—"haven't caused too much trouble."

"Ah, no." Gina laughed and gestured around her in a way that was completely Italian. "There is always more than enough in this house. Come," she said to the other two women, bobbing her head in encouragement and beckoning them forward.

"Adam"—he hadn't been called Adam since he was ten, and he wouldn't have corrected her for the world—"this is Tina, Angelo's wife." Tina was plump, with a madonna's face and shy smile. "And Pietro's wife, Marianna." Marianna was very pregnant, and had shrewd, laughing eyes.

"Hello," Marianna said, one hand at her waist.

"Hello," he said, including both of them.

She couldn't even be mad, Kate thought, feeling mad anyway. He was charming without knowing it, without effort. "I've brought basil," she said, moving to place it near the sink, trying to break the spell.

"*Ah, grazie, carina,*" Gina said. "Dinner will be in fifteen minutes. You can show your Adam the garden." She returned to the sink, then turned back around. "The peach tree, cara. Take a look at it for me, and if you find any left . . ."

Kate smiled gently as she took the basket from her mother. "*Sì,* Mama. And perhaps I should look at the roses?"

"If you like." Her mother smiled back. They understood each other. "Shears are in the basket."

Mac found himself staring at Kate. He had thought she couldn't get to him. He was wrong.

Trying to hide his thoughts, he met her eyes as she swung the basket mockingly. "Let me show you the garden," she cooed. "You can climb trees, can't you, Mac?" His face became a mask of tolerant suspicion, and the sound of muffled laughter followed them through the kitchen door.

The yard was a perfect expanse of green. Kate moved with purpose toward the trees at the far left, but Mac took time to look around. He could see a small herb garden at one end of the huge lawn, and a rambling, colorful design of rose bushes. The trees near Kate were orange, lemon, lime, peach, and something else. Pomegranate? Kate provided a beautiful, vivid contrast to the green trees, in a pale pink sweater above much faded Levi's.

"Hey." She turned suddenly, freeing that funny curl over her forehead. She nodded at a sturdy-limbed tree behind her. "Come give me a boost." She was so out of character, so childlike, she made him laugh.

"What are you smiling about, MacHugh? If I make you go up there, you'll break something." She grinned. "And I don't want to lose the peaches."

He stood close to her, wanting nothing so much as to release her golden hair and watch it tumble down, and kiss that sweet mouth.

When he didn't move she bent impatiently and placed the basket at the base of the tree. She turned back, her head just under his chin, and before she could make even a sound of protest, he lifted her off the ground, holding her against the tree and his wide chest.

"Mac," she singsonged in surprise.

"Did you know you have a cowlick, Katie Polanski?" he asked in a husky voice that sent a shiver of something unfamiliar through her. For a moment her mind was blank, her eyes wide and full of questions.

"I . . ." she started. "What . . ." Mac pressed her

more against the tree, using the length of his body to hold her. One hand shifted under her thighs to take some of her weight, the other moved to her forehead. Two of his fingers outlined the edge of that curl.

"Here," he whispered, staring into her eyes.

She had never seen the green in his eyes before, but now they seemed full of that color.

"I thought only little boys had cowlicks," he went on. He pulled on the curl gently, sending a prickling over her scalp and down her spine. He was going to kiss her.

"Mac . . ." she said without sound, her only protest. She didn't know if she wanted that kiss or not. He was strong, stronger than she had thought, and there was more chemistry between them than she had thought. His scent was fresh and warm and male, and Kate didn't know herself anymore. She looked straight ahead at his chest and saw her hands lying flat just beneath his shoulders. She could see the curling red-blond hairs at the vee of his sweater.

"Hypnosis," she mumbled, not realizing she had spoken aloud.

"I'm going to kiss you, Katie Polanski," Mac said, not taking his gaze from her mouth. Her breath changed with the beat of her heart. She felt the leap of his under her hand.

"But . . ." She moistened her lips and tried to shake her head. "I don't even"—his beautiful mouth was coming closer—"like you . . ." The last of her words escaped on a sigh as his lips touched hers. One kiss, and her mind was spinning crazily. She felt folded into him, surrounded, filled with the man, his scent, and a wildness she didn't understand. He had barely begun.

His mouth explored, then hungered as she answered him.

"Mac?" she asked finally against his lips, and he pulled back just enough to look into the pure blue of her eyes.

"Kiss me," he demanded tenderly. "Katie . . . kiss me." She moved, almost involuntarily at first, then deliberately, to touch his lips. He was still, waiting for her, barely containing the urgency he felt. Until she kissed him, he hadn't known how important it was to him that it be something she gave. He had only known he wanted it, wanted her.

Her lips moved silkily over his, shy, then warm. When his tongue touched hers, he groaned low and pressed closer. He could feel her breasts as if there weren't a scrap of cloth between them.

They explored each other's mouths, drinking in every taste and texture, the flavor of desire.

She made him forget time and place, and his hand had found its way to her waist and under the sweater before either of them even knew it happened. A tremor went through Kate when she felt the heat of his hand on her breast, and she moved closer.

The sound she made was nearly a sob, captured by his mouth. But it seemed he had only touched her when he jerked his hand away and put his head down on her shoulder. One of his thighs had come between hers and he could feel her warmth.

"Hold on," he gasped, his breathing harsh.

She felt bereft, and angry. She wanted him back.

"Oh, Katie." He laughed shakily, letting her slide down to the ground. "I never meant . . . We're in your mother's backyard."

She was still frowning, uncomprehending, when suddenly she realized what he had said. A noise caught in her throat and she looked around in panic.

"Anybody there?" he asked in a conspirator's voice, smiling crookedly. She shook her head, looking at him in a puzzled, vulnerable way that tugged at him.

She was trying desperately to remember exactly what had happened, what she had done, then he was hugging her, rocking her.

"I feel . . ." She put a hand over her eyes. "Drugged."

"I know," he said, still holding her. "I know."

When her hands wanted to move again on his chest, she drew away. "I've got to get the peaches," she murmured, "before my cousins come out here and shake you up." How could she laugh like this? Why did she feel so happy?

He looked skeptical. "No ladder?"

"Can you make a stirrup?" she asked. Reluctant, he obliged. She hardly thought the position of his hands was helpful, and said so. Mac played dumb.

"The basket," she said, holding out a hand. But before he gave it to her, he took her palm and kissed it softly.

"Don't fall," he said to her.

"Hmmf," she answered, and shimmied out on a limb, bracing herself carefully. The peaches were high, but they were perfect and worth the effort. Mac watched her like a hawk, and while it might have annoyed her yesterday, today she found it endearing.

"Catch." She dropped one below.

He caught it easily, took a bite, and said, "That leaves me only one hand."

"The thought terrifies me." She smiled, slipping the basket over her arm and dropping her legs to hang from a branch. One of his arms grabbed her around the waist, the other took the basket from her. "Where's your peach?" she asked, laughing.

"Right here," and he let her taste it on his mouth.

"Don't kiss me," she pleaded, tickling his lips.

"Okay," he said slowly, and kissed her again. "I'll stop now," he said, tasting each corner of her mouth. "Really." But when he licked her bottom lip, she was the one who deepened the kiss. Her hands fell on the soft hair at the base of his neck as she drew closer.

"No more," she said, throwing her head back. "Mac." He let his mouth fall to the base of her throat before he set her away from him. The look in his eyes stayed with her all the time she moved backward across the lawn.

It wasn't until later that Kate realized her mother had never asked about the roses.

# Four

The noise seemed deafening to Mac. Rossini was background music to the soprano scoldings of Tina and Marianna as they settled the three children at the table in the kitchen. Pietro argued the football game with Angelo in basso profundo. Then there was Gianetta. She was calm mezzo, giving instructions all around. Kate deserted Mac to help bring food from the kitchen. Her uncle Antonio sat, stern and silent, at one end of the table, eliminating any desire Mac might have had to speak.

In the face of this boisterous family, Mac was subdued and not a little off balance. Kate pretended not to notice.

Finally, the last chair shifted, the last warning was sent through the open kitchen door to the children's table, and Gianetta gave the signal to begin. Conversation never ceased as hands reached here and there over the table, and when Mac looked down he found enough food for three meals piled before him.

Gianetta had filled Mac's plate herself, thus announcing her approval to the family. Angelo filled Mac's glass to the brim with dry white wine and made a face at Kate across the table. Kate laughed back, and her cousins' wives looked at each other with grand significance.

Mac was having trouble swallowing as he remembered what might have been seen from any window at the back of the house. He didn't look up until he felt Kate nudge his knee with her own. They were all waiting for him. Pietro spoke again.

"You from Los Angeles?"

Mac swallowed the bite of fish he had taken. "We moved here when I was about sixteen. Before that, New York, Chicago, D.C. My father was a newspaperman." He frowned in concentration, then looked curiously at Pietro. "Sanducci. The Lakers." Pietro grinned. Mac gave a wide smile back. "Great game last week, Sandman."

"Thanks."

"Kate never said a word." Mac looked down at her wonderingly.

Pietro laughed, and spared a sly glance for Kate. "She never does." That was answered by a deep "Huh!" from the uncle. Pietro grunted as a woman's foot connected with his shin.

Tony made a great production of one sip of wine, then pointed his chin at Mac. "I am a locksmith." He seemed to be making some sort of challenge, but Mac had no idea what the proper response should be.

"Uncle Tony's the best locksmith in Los Angeles," Kate said quickly, pride and affection clear in her voice. Tony moved his head up and down as if he approved the statement and the moment hung in the air.

"This fish is fantastic, Mrs. Polanski," Mac said, turning to Gianetta.

She smiled regally, and corrected him. "Gina."

"Gina," Mac repeated, ignoring the fierce look from the head of the table.

Tony waved his fork toward Kate. "So, somebody hit you, Katerina?" All eyes turned to Mac, who lost his ability to swallow.

"Uncle Tony!" Kate laughed at him, shaking her head. "I bit my lip when I bumped my head. An accident."

The tension subsided as Gina took a look at the injury and Marianna quickly changed the subject. "What story are you working on this week, Kate?"

"Nothing much. I'm still working on that preschool scandal. They keep throwing out the testimonies of the children, and now there's talk that the D.A. wants to reduce the charges." She went on about the particulars of the case, very conscious of Mac beside her. But she never mentioned that they were working together.

After dinner Mac talked to Pietro about the next basketball game the Lakers were scheduled to play while he and Kate helped little Mike make a yarn toy for his kitten.

Mac sat in the passenger seat, his back against the door, as they drove to Beverly Hills. Kate was concentrating, and he wanted to accustom himself to the look of her, even if it meant letting her play race car. It amazed him that so much could change in the space of a few hours. But now he remembered times he had caught himself watching her, times he had admired a story of hers, and he felt warmed by the other facets of Kate Polanski. He liked her, more than liked her. He felt elated and ridiculously possessive, and he couldn't wait until he could arrange to have her alone in a setting of his choice.

Kate drew in the scent of jasmine, annoyed by its romance. She frowned mightily through the windshield as she tried to hide the confusion she was feeling. She was having second thoughts, and he was sitting so that one of his knees touched the outside of her thigh. She was determined he wouldn't see she was aware of it.

What was happening to her, to them? It had certainly never been her intention to become involved with Adam MacHugh. The timing couldn't be worse. And now she was caught by desires she didn't even want to admit.

It was just a physical attraction, she thought, giving him a quick glance. But, she thought, smiling to herself, physical attraction was a wonderful thing.

Ah, but to him this was probably a matter of routine seduction. Her hands clenched on the wheel. She chanced another look his way and saw he was still staring at her. Would it be worth it to find out? Did she even have a choice?

Whether it was the thrill of the chase or chemistry, she knew he wanted her. He made no secret of it. And she was certainly not immune. He made her feel happy for no reason at all.

"Is your father still alive?"

She jumped at the question. It was the last she had expected, and it took her a moment to regain her composure.

"I never knew my father." Relax, be casual, she told herself. "What's yours like? Are you close?"

"Oh, yeah, he's a great guy." Mac shook his head. "As soon as I talked him into retiring, he took a full-time teaching job at USC." He lifted a brow and tried to contain his grin. "Your uncle seems to take a pretty fatherly interest in you."

"Yes." She laughed warmly. "And isn't he subtle?"

"Mmm. I guess I'm lucky; he would have thought it bad manners to bring the shotgun to the table."

"He believes if he starts out tough, he can keep the prospects in line," she said, then blushed fiery red at the implication in her words.

She started when she felt the touch of Mac's thumb, brushing a wisp of hair behind her ear. "Easy." The caress lingered, trailing down the side of her neck to rest there.

"You're distracting me," she said with a shake of her head, her tone businesslike.

"I like that," he countered.

She tried again. "Look, Mac—"

"Shh." His thumb moved back and forth over her collarbone. "No warnings, no explanations. It's too soon for either." He waited until she stopped at a light. "I'll just take this." And he bent to press his warm mouth to the place he had touched. Her response was completely involuntary. She would never have leaned into him, but it seemed her bones were melting away.

Someone behind her honked impatiently and she jerked back, pushing the car into gear, her bottom lip caught between her teeth. Mac settled into his seat, a smile playing about his lips. Kate concentrated on traffic.

"I like your mother," Mac said. "She has a way about her. Kindness and quiet strength."

"She's a very loving woman." Kate laughed. "She's ruled that house and everyone in it for years, and not one of us could tell you how she always gets her way. But she usually does. Even Uncle Tony bows when she gets that look on her face." She glanced at Mac, showing her surprise. "She certainly liked *you . . . Adam.*"

"I seem to have that effect on women." His tone was bland.

Kate waved her fist at him.

"I still get a kick out of this little Italian woman having a name like Polanski. Divorced?"

"No." The answer was clipped. Mac eased back in his seat, noting the tension that came with the question.

"I want to make a stop, drop off some film, okay?" she asked.

"Sure," he answered, and moments later she pulled up to a small white house on a quiet side street.

"Just be a minute," she said, and she took her purse with her to the door. Mac saw one of the photographers from the paper answer the door. He relaxed. Kate was back a few seconds later, and they were on their way.

When she pulled up before the Mexican restaurant and bar, she turned to Mac and gave a long sigh.

"I would love it if you would wait here," she began, raising her hand to forestall the automatic protest, "but twice in two days is really too much to ask." His look was trouble. "So," she asked with a winsome expression, "could you be a distant customer?" Her clear blue eyes blinked once. "Please?"

Last Thursday he wouldn't have had a single qualm about turning her down. "A less than distant customer," he conceded.

Her smile was quick and bright.

She gave him two and a half minutes before she walked into the bar. It was twilight gray after the light outside. The air smelled of coffee and bacon, liquor and cigarettes. Mac sat three stools down with a new beer.

She walked to a solitary seat, lodged her purse near her feet, and assumed the air of a woman on leisure time.

"Brian," she said, nodding to the dark-haired bartender.

"The beautiful Kate," he said, managing to saunter the two steps he took to reach her. He leaned against the bar with both hands. "Where you been? Rudolf's been asking about you."

She grinned. "You tell Rudolf he's too old for me, but I send him a kiss anyway."

"Put it here." Brian pointed happily to his right cheek.

"Uh-uh." Kate shook her head and resisted the impulse to glance at Mac. "You're much more dangerous than old Rudolf."

Brian liked that. "What can I get you, Kate?"

"Well . . ." She leaned her chin on one hand. "I'm working." She waited for Brian to nod. "You know a detective named Jarré?"

"Yeah, Guy Jarré. He's French, or was. Been with this division a few years. He's usually attached to the Crime Prevention unit." He set a glass of club soda with lime in front of her. "He comes here after work a couple times a week. Drinks wine. One, two, then home." Brian wiped the bar. "Gets along with most of the guys. Knows a lot of the French merchants in Beverly Hills."

Kate pulled her purse to her lap and took out a small yellowed newswire photograph. "Ever see this man?"

Brian took the picture from her and cocked a brow. "Maybe with Jarré?" Kate suggested.

"Don't think so." Brian shook his head.

"He's got gray hair now."

Brian took another look. "No."

Kate took out a new photograph. "How about him?"

"Yeah." Brian leaned one hand on the bar and rubbed the other over his beard. "He came in looking for Jarré last week. They left together."

"Did you happen to hear any of the conversation?"

Brian shrugged. "Sorry, Kate."

"Thanks, Brian." She slid off the stool. "Could you give me a call if you see this guy again?" She handed Brian the picture.

"Sure, Kate. You playin' next summer?"

"Wouldn't miss it."

"Great. I'll tell Rudolf you send your love."

Kate laughed over her shoulder. "Do that."

Mac took her arm in a firm grip when he caught up with her outside. "I want to talk to you," he growled, dragging her between buildings. Before she could even register surprise, he kissed her until her arms wound about his neck.

"Just checking," he said against her lips and made her smile. "Who's Rudolf?"

She kissed his sandpapery chin, his tender mouth. "Wouldn't you like to know?"

He grabbed a handful of her soft honey-colored hair and gently pulled down, forcing her head back. His lips, then his teeth grazed her neck. Her eyes closed and a shiver traced her spine. Then his hands pressed her closer still.

"Katie," he whispered at her ear, before his mouth touched the sensitive skin behind it. "What was I mad about?"

She pulled far enough away to look into the green-gold of his eyes, then at his mouth. "I don't care." And the kiss he gave her was rich and warm and wonderfully dangerous.

"Brian is a friend of Angelo's," she said when she could. "We all play softball in the summer. Rudolf is his basset hound." She kissed a corner of his mouth. "Is that what you wanted to know?"

"Mm." He stopped the kiss. "Whose picture did he recognize?"

"Ferranti's chauffeur." Her hands traced Mac's sleek brows, the smooth temples, and around his ears to slide through his hair. She couldn't understand the feeling it gave her to touch this man, but somehow it moved her, gentling her heart, tossing her careful plans to the wind.

He looked into her eyes for a moment, then released her hair and pulled her back onto the sidewalk with an arm about her waist.

"You have to let me drive," he said, not looking at her as they walked to the car.

"I *have* to let you?"

"You want my hands on you or the wheel?"

"Oh."

He loved to watch the color come and go in her cheeks.

"I have to finish some research at the paper," Mac said as he drove her home. "Can I call you later?" She didn't say a word, didn't smile, but she nodded yes.

He parked her car in the small drive and pulled the emergency brake. Kate felt strangely reluctant to move. Her movements seemed slow, awkward, as she got out of the car and slammed the door. Mac walked her to the back gate. One hand reaching for the latch, she turned to meet his eyes.

"How will you get there?" she asked.

He studied her solemn expression. "I've got Rob's car."

An evening breeze pushed a strand of her hair over one brow. Her hand moved away from the gate and to her temple, smoothing the hair back. Mac continued staring at her. There was a moment of tension, of expectation between them. Then she saw his chest rise and fall quickly as he put his hands on her shoulders, pulling her to him. His thumbs rubbed back and forth.

Looking up, she noticed the line of a tiny scar just under his chin. Her eyes closed as he leaned forward. With slow tenderness, he kissed one arching brow, the other, the corners of her mouth. Her lips parted, and her hands found his hard waist. She could feel the warmth of his body through his sweater.

His mouth brushed hers gently, twice, then he was lifting her up and into him with a fierce, stunning hunger. She felt his heart beating under her hand as his tongue explored her mouth, and her hands tightened. There was a blackness behind her eyes and a rushing excitement in her veins when she finally felt his hand on her breast, and she leaned into his touch.

Her hands slid under his sweater so she could touch the warm silk of his skin. Her fingers ran over the smooth muscles of his back, up and over his shoulder blades. His mouth moved on hers more urgently until finally he pulled back with a low groan, still caressing her arms, her shoulders. He dropped his head, and she could feel the heat of his breath fanning her neck. Her own head fell to one side, and he hesitated, then let his lips lightly touch the soft skin of her throat before he drew away.

He looked into her eyes and let his breathing slow. "I'll call around ten," he said. He touched her cheek, then turned to go. Kate didn't watch him. She hurried into the yard, closed the gate with one palm, and rested her forehead against the hard wood, breathing fast.

She thought about him all evening, the trick he had of looking away into the corners of a room, the way he took his time before he spoke, the husky sound of his laughter. And every time she caught herself thinking of him, she would slowly shake her head.

He was the last thing she needed, but she couldn't seem to remember that when he was touching her. She wasn't a woman who lost control; it was not a feeling she relished. But the worst was the fear that she no longer had a choice, that the decision had somehow been taken from her.

At one point she started toward the kitchen, and once there couldn't remember what she had wanted. Three minutes later, she was wearing a track in the living room rug, her gaze drawn to the phone again and again. Finally, with a huff of exasperation, she went to the closet for her jacket. She needed to walk.

It was late by the time she finally got home. The phone was ringing as she opened the door, and she realized she had forgotten to turn on her machine. Ignoring the sound, she took her time hanging up her jacket. The ringing only made her angry. Why was this happening to her? Why this man? Why now?

She pushed at the closet door, turned, and walked to the wall behind the phone. It took only seconds to find and unplug the connection. Then she put on the kettle and went to her bedroom. Dragging her notes from her purse, she dropped them on the bed, pulled a nightgown from the drawer, and changed quickly.

An hour later, she pushed the notes off her lap and let her head fall back. She listened to the silence for a few minutes before reaching for the lamp switch. She *would* sleep. She would.

Kate didn't wake up until seven-ten the next morning when her alarm went off. It was raining outside, without a break in the sky. She saw on the news that it had been pouring all night. She had coffee and toast in perfect imitation of her normal routine, and refused to think of what the first sight of Adam MacHugh might do to her resolve.

She got to work early, looking straight down the aisle as the elevator door opened. Her first step out of the car was cautious, the next more certain. She didn't see his coat on the long rack, and by the time she had settled at her desk she was fine. Then she saw the envelope.

It was white, business-size, and addressed simply "Kate." She looked over her right shoulder quickly, but Mac's desk was empty. She opened the envelope. The message was one line, handwritten on a scrap of memo paper. *"Where were you?"*

"Last night," Mac finished aloud, from behind her left shoulder. She jumped. He bent his knee to nudge her chair sideways until her leg pressed lightly against his. The subtle scent of her perfume drifted up to him and his gaze followed the line of the thin gold chain she wore around her neck. It was weighted with a tiny gold nugget that lay against her delicate breastbone. His smile was bright and teasing. "Mornin', Katie."

She looked back down immediately. Her face felt hot. "Hello, Mac." When she moved her leg, he pushed on the swivel chair until, again, there was contact.

"Hey," he said softly. "You okay?"

She hesitated a moment, staring at where her thigh touched his calf. "I'm fine."

He read her tone perfectly. The night that had passed had changed things. He moved his leg away. "There's something different here." He took a good look at her. "Last night?" he asked in a different tone.

"I was out." She finally raised her eyes to his. Hers were distant.

"You two are here early," Rob said, and Kate welcomed the interruption. "What's goin' on?"

Mac looked up, frowning, and shrugged. Rob pursed his lips, stared at Kate's frowning face, then moved on down the aisle.

"I have to get to work, Mac," Kate said.

Mac gave her a long look, said, "Unfinished business," and walked back to his own desk.

Somehow Kate made it through the first hour of phone calls, then Joe yelled for her. There were mud slides in the canyons.

The rains came twice a year, late fall and early spring. The mud slides that came with them were a California nightmare for homeowners. The ground could fall away with very little warning, and a house that was safe one year might be in danger the next. People in the hills used sheets of plastic and cement shoring, but even that didn't always prevent a slide.

Joe sent Kate alone with instructions to get pictures if there was anything dramatic, but this was the beginning of the season. The damage should be minimal.

She took the freeway up to Hollywood Boulevard, then made her way to Nichols Canyon. About half a mile up, there was a roadblock. Kate was stopped because her car was too lightweight. The patrolman nodded when he saw her press pass, but asked if Kate could grab a ride with one of the media vans when they came through. She agreed and parked on the shoulder. Then she clamped her laminated press pass to the lapel of her trench coat, grabbed her camera, and flagged down a television van with her notebook.

The rain was blinding and seemed to muffle everything. She had to yell through the noise of the rain. *"L.A. Daily."* She put a thumb under her pass with her picture. "Can you take me up?"

The van door opened almost immediately. "C'mon in." Channel Seven's crew made her very welcome. There was a quick scramble, a few teasing comments about lending hands and swimming lessons, and she was in the back of the van. She shared a bench with the minicam, and the man and the woman in the back and the two men up front quickly introduced themselves.

The highway patrolman stopped them for the standard warnings; to stay on the main road, not to take chances, or stray from the van, and to leave when signaled by firemen or patrolmen. Then they were waved on. When they reached the highest point on the first hill, they stopped.

These people were professionals, Kate noted. They piled out of the van with precision speed, looking for anything out of the ordinary. They didn't have to look very long.

# Five

"Oh, my God," the woman next to Kate said, staring down. "Danny, get the camera over here. You won't believe it."

Kate didn't believe it, either, though she was already working with her own camera. She lifted it and followed the line of the ravine—a ravine that hadn't been there yesterday. It went on for almost half a mile. In some places, backyards were missing. Kate could see a pool that had cracked and caved in and was sliding downward. But the worst hit were the homes near the hill. The first one had collapsed under the weight of the mud; half of the second was gone. She shot a whole roll of film.

Kate let her camera swing lightly against her stomach as she checked her footing and found a boulder to stand on for a bit more height. From that vantage point, she could see two helicopters, three giant red trucks, and men fanning out over the area.

Pulling her steno pad from her waistband, she held one edge of her coat over it as she took notes. Five minutes passed, maybe ten.

When Kate was finished with her notes she looked across the blacktop. The television crew was just beginning to film, and after a few minutes Kate grew impatient. She could get a quick interview with one of the firemen and still make deadline if she was lucky, but not if she couldn't get off this hill.

She looked behind her speculatively. She was only a mile or so from her car, and only two blocks from the first fire truck.

"Thanks for the ride up, guys," she called. "I'll find a way back down there." Kate wasn't surprised when they waved her on. They had their own story to shoot. She looked down at the running shoes she had put on this morning and grimaced. The fastest way to the slides was through the brush. Well, at least she was wearing gloves.

She reached the first house and saw that the damage looked much worse down here than it had from above. She found a fireman taking a quick coffee break and persuaded him to give her the information she needed. There was one death, he told her. Two people had been injured, but not critically. She took names. The damage could be estimated at about ten million dollars.

Kate checked her watch, thinking she might have time to get to the hospital if she hurried. When she looked up the fireman had gone back to work. She had to get to a phone.

She half walked, half ran along the soft shoulder of the road, heading back toward her car. She was passed by an ambulance and a police car going the wrong direction. They were driving down the center of the canyon road and Kate knew they'd have trouble seeing her in the gray light. She stepped farther out of the way.

Then, without warning, she was falling, arms flailing wildly, calling out, and all she could think was that she hoped her camera would stay dry inside her coat. She tried to grab for brush, but it was falling with her. She rolled over twice and landed painfully in the mud, face down.

Her heart was pounding furiously as she braced herself slowly, waiting to see if she would fall farther. But there she stayed. Looking up, she could see that she had only fallen about twelve feet. Curling her feet under her, she sat up and caught her breath. She was okay, everything was okay.

She took a minute longer to check the condition of her camera and notebook before she started the climb up. They were dry, though her flash attachment was missing. She could only hope her film wasn't damaged. Ten minutes later she was back on the road, and she had to laugh when she looked down at herself.

That was how the Channel Seven truck found her, covered in pounds of black mud and laughing in the rain.

"On-the-spot reporting," she said into the open window. The sliding door opened, she was pulled in, and a towel was pushed into her hands.

She was still smiling when she slushed out of the elevator and made her way to Joe's office. After a few explicit exclamations, he sat her down, dragged off her coat, sloshed brandy into a cup of coffee, and stood over her while she sipped and told him what had happened. Then he extracted her camera and notes and put her in front of his own computer terminal while he took her camera to the lab.

Kate was two paragraphs into the story when she was pulled right out of her chair and into Mac's arms.

"Katie!" His voice was low and harsh, but he was warm, so warm. "Katie, are you all right?"

She couldn't help the sigh, he felt so good. But she was full of mud, and told him so.

"I don't give a damn about your mud, are you all right?" He was nearly shouting now.

"I'm fine, Mac." She smiled at him. "I fell down, but I'm fine."

"You look like hell." He cradled her face in one hand, wiping away a bit of dirt. Then he kissed her sweetly, just once. "Are you sure you aren't hurt?"

She closed her eyes. "Mmm-hmm."

His lips brushed hers again. "You on deadline?"

"Mmm-hmm."

"Then?" His thumbs stroked her cheeks.

"Joe promised me a shower upstairs," she said softly.

"We have to talk, Kate." It wasn't a question. That was when Kate wondered why she was fighting him.

"All right."

He pushed her hair out of her eyes and let her go. "I'll see you later," he said as he left her, and she never got a chance to tell him about the smudge of dirt on his cheek.


Kate left Joe to his editing and found the old jeans and sweater she kept in her bottom desk drawer. Mac didn't look up from his computer, but she *knew* he knew she was there. Then she took the service elevator up to the executive shower. It was white; white tile, white soap, white towels, and steaming hot water. There were only three bruises that she could count in the wide mirror, but, drying off, Kate was suddenly very, very tired.

Back at her desk, she couldn't concentrate. She sat at her terminal and pretended to write while she watched Mac work. He caught her twice, but she looked away too quickly to be caught a third time. When she looked up again, he was on his way to Joe's office. He came back with a strange look in his eye.

"Let's go," he said, pulling back her chair. Kate tilted her head at him, but decided it wasn't worth the question. It didn't matter where.

She shut down her terminal, got her purse and her abused camera, and followed Mac to the elevator. They both looked straight ahead, without touching, on the way down.

The rain had stopped and the streets were black and shiny, but the sun was beginning to burn the clouds away. Kate and Mac still didn't speak as they walked to her car. Mac moved to the passenger door and held out his hand for the keys. Kate handed them over, and when he motioned her in, she got in. He only drove a few blocks before he pulled into a parking place and parked. He took a breath, and let it out slowly.

"What happened last night, Kate?" he asked quietly. "I know . . . I know you felt what I did. What happened? What changed?"

She couldn't answer for a long time. She tried to find the words to explain, but she could only bite her lip and shake her head. Finally, she turned to look at him, to say *something*, and the concern and worry in his green-gold eyes took her breath away.

She smiled. "Oh, Mac. I was afraid." Her smile widened. "I'm not anymore."

He reached for her hand.


He drove to Malibu, one hand cradling hers most of the way.

"Where are you taking me?" she asked.

"A place I know where the sound of the waves will hypnotize you into telling me all your deepest, darkest . . ."

"Mmm." She withheld her smile and looked out her window. "Do we take turns?"

He gave her an odd look. "Fair is fair."

"Good."

They turned left onto a little road that ran behind the beach houses. Mac drove almost to its end before he pulled over to park on the sandy shoulder. When they got out of the car Kate assumed they would cross to the beach between the buildings, but Mac led her to the rear door of a two-story house. Reaching behind a bush, he pulled out a small metal box. The box held a key.

"Of course," he said, glancing at her over one shoulder, "I could have let you open it, couldn't I?"

Kate concentrated on the blue of the sky. Mac opened the door, leaning against it so that she had to brush his chest to pass.

"That's a cheap trick, MacHugh," she announced, when she was under his chin, "and becoming overused."

"Just when I was getting fond of it." He grinned and planted a kiss on the tip of her nose. With a small shove Kate freed herself.

"This isn't yours," she said walking into an off-white entryway. "Oh . . ." She looked around and down stairs that led to a living area bounded by sheer glass walls. The house was shiny new; white walls and blond wood. It was bare, undecorated, unpolished. It was wonderful.

"Oh, Mac." She turned back to him in delight. His smile made her turn again and rush down the stairway. She crossed the room to the window, placing her hands on the cool glass. She stared out, mesmerized, until she realized that Mac was just behind her. He reached out to the right, unlocking the sliding door there, and the smell of the ocean came in with the quick breeze.

Kate breathed deeply of the warm scent.

"It's almost finished," he said quietly. "Just a bit of sanding left upstairs."

"Then it *is* yours?" She turned to him, eyes wide.

"There is a mortgage." His voice evinced amusement.

She laughed up at him. "And I thought all you did in your spare time was chase strippers."

"Very funny."

"Really." She looked around, taking in the vaulted ceiling, the sense of light and space. "It's a lovely house, Mac."

He gave a little bow of acknowledgment and tugged on her hand until they were in the middle of the room. "Down," he commanded, a light in his eyes.

"Down?" She looked doubtfully around her.

A big hand covered the top of her head and pushed downward until she sat on the floor. "Now." He smiled, settling himself beside her. "Ask."

"Ask what?"

"All those things you haven't asked."

He looked so smug, she almost didn't, but she decided on a better revenge. Eyes veiled, she began in rapid fire.

"Where did you get the money for this house? Why are you suddenly interested in me? Is it just habit? Are you really as much a chauvinist as you seem? Do you gloat over women with the boys in the locker room? Have you ever been married? If not, why not? How did you get that little scar under your chin?"

Breathless, she stopped for air. But she had hardly taken a lungful before Mac grabbed her arms and dragged her up against him. His chest was hard warmth. His mouth opened over hers in a kiss that was searing and sweet.

"Anything else?" he asked.

"Do you talk in bed?"

His eyes laughed into hers. "You get away with murder."

"You have the most beautiful mouth"—she touched a corner with one finger—"and eyes"—she caressed a brow. "This face." She shook her head in wonder. "You almost make me jealous." Her fingers traced a cheek as his skin reddened.

"Stop." He was embarrassed.

She took her hand from his face, but he grabbed it back and kissed it softly. "Don't stop that."

"I don't know." She studied his face, then looked into his bright eyes. "I feel like I'm out of control." Her lashes fell. "Do you?"

Again his mouth met hers.

A few minutes later he said between kisses, "My mother's father left me the money for the house." He pulled on her bottom lip with his teeth. "I fell out of a tree when I was six." He nuzzled her cheek with his and nipped at her ear. "I have never been married because I never felt the urge." Then he pulled back far enough to stare into the sea-blue of her eyes. "I don't broadcast the details of my private life. I don't know if I'm a chauvinist or not. I find I think about you all the time; the way you move and smile, the things you say, and I don't know why. What else did you ask me?"

"That's all." She couldn't look away from him as his mouth came closer.

"I'm glad you like my mouth," he said against her lips, "because I love yours." Just before the kiss deepened he drew back one more time. "Oh, and . . ." His hands slid over her shoulders and down her arms to take her waist and hold her tightly to him. "Sometimes I talk . . ." There was nothing casual about this kiss, and both hearts raced. "Sometimes I don't."

He pressed her down so that she was lying beneath him, her back on the polished floor. Her eyes were wide and dark with wonder and a thousand lover's questions. His were tender and bright with desire.

"It's happening so fast," she said breathlessly.

"I know." He smoothed the curl from her face. Strangely, that gentle touch reassured her, and she reached up to mark the indentation of his rough chin.

"You want me," she whispered, and it was half a question.

"Yes." His voice was sure.

"Here?" This was the moment of decision. A wrong word or move . . .

"Anywhere." His eyes held hers, telling her he felt what she did. A beginning.

Sense was forgotten, and control. He bent to place his lips lightly at her throat, his hands beneath her shoulders, raising her. And Kate knew that if all were lost tomorrow, today she wanted this.

Now that he was certain of her, he wanted to weigh the time, to fill every second with pleasure, to test this strange bonding.

Kate was drugged with the quality of his touch, the ways he spoke to her through hands and lips. She sighed in answer. His hands lowered her again to the floor and he pulled at the old-fashioned pins that held her hair until it slipped to her shoulders. He rubbed it between his fingers and pursued its length, combing it over her shoulders with his fingers. The curls ended just above her breasts.

Mac looked at her questioningly. Her smile answered him quickly, and her eyes darkened even more as he leaned forward to inhale the new scent. He rubbed his face against the soft gold of her hair. His lips moved down to kiss the longest curl and then her breast. Kate gasped and reached to hold him to her as he bit lightly through the thickness of her sweater. She turned her face away and closed her eyes to keep the feeling. Then his hands were at her waist, fingers trailing slow designs under the sweater, up and over her ribs.

She held her breath as his palms brushed against her breasts. His hands were wide, covering her easily, rough in texture, but most gentle. Her breathing quickened.

He rested on his elbows, lying between her legs. The hard heat of him against her was erotic, exciting. She could only wait and watch the changes in his face. It was warm with color, soft with passion, and so very human.

Unsteady hands pulled at sweaters, up and over, and they paused to press flesh to flesh. His shoulders were broad and tanned, his chest firm, covered in patterns of red-blond curls. Kate laughed at the friction. She felt so happy.

He drew away to look at her. Now he could trace with his eyes where his hands had touched. Her skin was petal-soft, her breasts round and pale. He mapped them with his tongue, then closed his lips on her, smiling at the sounds she made.

Her nails scraped lightly over him. He ran the backs of his hands up her arms, over her shoulders, down her ribs. One hand stroked her through her tight jeans as his lips and teeth teased her breast. His breath ragged, he pulled away. Then he kissed her mouth again and again as if nothing were enough.

He was lost in a pleasure so sharp, so full. His world was changed by this woman. His hips moved in a rhythm echoed by his tongue. Again she answered. But now the pleasure was almost pain and both needed more.

One of his large hands had unfastened her jeans as he kissed her and he was quick to slip beneath the silky panties to her warmth. Her legs parted in unconscious invitation and a low sound came from his throat at the perfect feel of her.

Kate swallowed, trembling, and pulled a strand of his hair. Mac looked up and stopped to kiss her reassuringly. His eyes caressed her. Then he tugged the rest of her clothing down and stood, his hands at his belt. He stripped quickly and again their bodies met, rolling until she lay atop him.

They laughed, and kissed until she pushed back to run her hands and gaze down his length. Her hands molded his shoulders; heated skin and hard muscle. Her breath caught as she sensed the power in the man, restrained for her sake. She followed the path of curls and touched him, uncertain, eager.

"Kate." His fingertips grazed her cheek and her eyes sought his. "This . . . It's something rare. Do you feel it?"

She smiled and put her arms far around him, resting her body against his. "I want to hold all of you." She laughed. "To have you too."

"Kate." The whisper turned to passion.


She was aware of many things as she lay there, arms above her head, her back against the sun-warmed wood. The smell of the sea mixed with the scents of man. Sunset splashed the sky with brilliant reds.

The air was cooling now, but was still thick with moisture. It caressed her fevered skin. She was aware of the slowing of her breath and Mac's. Strongest was the feeling of completeness, of contentment. Mac was stretched out beside her, his face against her neck, his legs tangled with hers. His fingers caressed where there was contact.

Emotion burned behind her eyes. In her mind, she took a picture of his moment, so that later she might cull the memory and savor this feeling.

"You talked," she mused, staring into the great height of the beamed ceiling.

"Mmm." He raised up on one elbow and leaned down to kiss her navel. It caved in. "I'm glad you noticed." Her stomach quivered with laughter.

She sighed, breathless. "I can't move."

"Don't try."

"Mac . . ."

# *Six*

They were silent on the way back to Kate's house, each fearing what the other might say as the world intruded.

Mac did not consider himself an emotional man. He was a reporter. He dealt in facts, not bias, not feelings. Until nine months ago, when he had first met a woman named Elizabeth, his associations with the opposite sex had usually followed a pattern; casual interest followed by casual acquaintance, then casual sex.

Mac was aware that there were women who wanted to go to bed with him, some who liked to be seen with him, and a few who just enjoyed being around him. He knew what he looked like, how women reacted. Sometimes it was convenient, sometimes embarrassing. That was why his close friends were men.

Of course, Elizabeth had been friend as well as lover. Elizabeth wasn't traditionally beautiful, but she was so natural and at ease with herself and her looks that you believed her to be beautiful. She was a lanky brunette and wonderfully talented. A concert pianist with a dust-dry sense of humor and a sailor's vocabulary. She and Mac had taken to each other immediately but, even after five months together, they couldn't progress past *like*.

It was Elizabeth who had showed Mac he could expect more from the women he knew, that a relationship should be full of more than good sex and simple conversation. She was still one of his dearest friends.

Now there was Katerina Polanski. She, too, was talented, but she was very different. Unpredictable, quick, somehow innocent, she didn't flirt. She didn't tease. And she drew more emotion from him than any woman he'd ever known. He didn't begin to understand her, but somehow that mattered very little. Mac knew instinctively that what she responded to was inside him.

While Mac drove, Kate struggled to push her thoughts away and let her instincts guide her. Once before, she had been involved with a charming, handsome man. Michael had been an attorney who was contending for judicial appointment. He had believed that cultivating certain women was the quickest road; something Kate found out too late.

Yet here she was, letting herself be interested in Adam MacHugh. She wasn't one for one-night stands, or casual affairs. But even knowing it was unlike her, she had said yes today. And she would again. Her responses to Mac frightened her. She was sure she hadn't the experience to handle a man like him. She didn't think he had a great deal of respect for women in general. Nonetheless, watching his hands on the wheel of her car, remembering the tenderness, the caring and the passion of the last hours, she knew she would take her chances.

When he turned into her driveway he stopped the car, and every movement was weighted, deliberate.

"Don't ask me to go." His voice was gruff. He glared at the dashboard.

"I don't want you to go," Kate answered, watching his expression lighten. She put her hand on his thigh, then felt the pressure of his hand over hers.

"I have this feeling," he said, "that when I leave, one of us will back away." He turned to face her.

"Not me, Adam MacHugh," she said quietly. "I knew from the moment you walked into my house Sunday morning that something important was happening. And I wanted it." She saw his eyes darken and lifted her chin. "I might have been after you months ago if you weren't treating me like a cross between a cub reporter and a dim debutante."

"What?" His head snapped back in surprise.

"You did." He tried to get a word in but Kate mowed right over him. "You'd stare at my legs and then go chase other women."

He laughed. "I don't chase women."

Kate blushed, amazed at her own vehemence.

Mac picked up the hand he held and placed a soft kiss on her palm. "No one has legs like yours," he said. He was remembering stroking them an hour ago.

"Mac."

"Mmm?"

"It is more than that?"

In an instant he was serious. He gazed at her face, into her eyes. He touched her cheek. "I've never known anyone like you." A fingertip brushed the soft skin. "Bright. Independent. Mysterious. I want to know all of it. But you have to understand . . ." He paused dramatically. "The way you look"—he smiled, she fell—"does me in."

"You do know just what to say to a girl." She

sighed and tilted her head toward the house. "Let's go in. I'll scrub your back."

"The idea has possibilities." He let her drag him along to the front gate, then to the door. He used her keys to open it, then pressed them into her palm.

Inside, he watched her walk over the thick carpet, through her small house. She was pulling her sweater up from her waist, her arms crossed in front of her.

"Mac?" She dropped one arm to beckon over her shoulder as she reached her bedroom door. She had the beginning of a dimple he had never noticed, and he thought that he would remember this moment when he was eighty. It was the moment he knew he was lost to love.

"Well, *come on,*" she said, and disappeared inside.

He grinned and followed.

Her bedroom was decorated in palest shades of sand, rose, and green. There were lush plants in every corner, brass accents on wallframes and bedside tables. Over the bed an embroidered golden dragon glittered from a four-foot framed section of mauve silk. There were mirrors on the large double closet, reflecting colors and the bed. Despite the shine of the dragon and the brass, it was a subtle room, softly lit, romantic without lace. Like Kate.

"Where are you?" she called as she came out of the bathroom. She had on the white robe he had seen her in yesterday morning, a thousand years ago. Golden hair fell all to one side. She was tying the belt at her waist, her head at an inquiring angle. "What are you doing?" she said softly.

"Learning you." He stood there, his eyes holding hers, then he smiled a slow smile. He watched her expression and shortened the distance between them with two long strides. When he raised his hands to her, she was statue still. His thumbs brushed her cheeks, then traced the line of her neck. "Your skin looks like mother-of-pearl." She arched to his touch, and his hands slid down over her shoulder blades as he pulled her close. "And smells so *woman*."

Her pulse raced as she felt the heat pour in waves from his body to hers. Drawing back, she lifted her mouth to his.

He burned her with his kiss, his hands. His tongue explored her and she was anxious, needing more than just touch, more than the moment.

He broke away, and she saw in his eyes that he felt it, too, and that it had surprised him the way an electric shock surprises. It seemed a long time before he moved, bending again to her lips, this time with a tentative touch. One corner, then the other. She sighed as she felt the rasp of his cheek, knew he was breathing in the scent of her skin. Suddenly, Kate understood that this man had the power to change her life, her future. Her hands began to shake, then her body. With a start, she tried to pull away.

His arms tightened around her in a hard embrace, and he rocked her gently, one hand in her hair. "Shh, Katie. Shh."

She kept her face buried in his chest as she willed the shaking to stop. But it seemed forever before she could control the tremors.

When he felt her begin to relax Mac put one hand on her slender neck and tried to turn her head up, but she twisted farther to hide her face.

"Katie, look at me." His voice was so gentle.

She shook her head against him.

He kissed the top of her head, then in one smooth motion scooped her into his arms. Her head fell against his chest as he walked to the bed, and he sat down with her in his lap.

"You okay?" he asked after a minute or two of just holding her.

She nodded cautiously. "I don't know . . ." She shook her head.

He hugged her, then stood up with her still in his arms.

"Where are we going?" she asked.

He smiled down at her. "I'm going to find the shower." The expression he wore became very scientific. "I want to see what you look like under water."

Kate let him take her into the bathroom, set her on her feet, open the door to the shower, and turn on the jets of water. All the while, she studied him. He was wonderful to watch. He caught her staring and began to take off his clothes, grinning wickedly.

Neither spoke.

He reached out one hand and hooked it in the sash of her robe, pulling so that she had to lean against him. She felt the robe fall away, then felt his bare flesh.

Lifting her by the waist, he walked her over the step into the large rectangular shower stall. The water was warm, soothing. Mac held her there, beneath the water, until it ran in streams down her body. She turned her head one way and the other as her hair got soaked.

Mac took the soap, gliding it between his hands in slow motions until it lathered. Then he rolled it over her shoulders and neck with sliding fingers.

Never had she felt more female to male. Never had she been so aware of every nerve, of skin and muscle and bone, as she was with him.

With his hands he learned her: ankles, knees, hands, breasts, and thighs. He rubbed his body against hers, and his fingers shimmered over her, then his lips.

Kate struggled to keep her mind clear, not to lose herself in him.

He kissed the fist her hand had made, then kissed her velvet throat. Finally, he whispered, "Want me, Kate. Tremble for me. Need me." And with his last words she have a cry and reached out for him.

Impatient, he turned her under the water to rinse away the soap. He twisted the faucet to off and pushed open the glass door before raising her in his arms. Dripping wet, his skin glistening in the lamplight, he took her to her bed and laid her on the pale rose comforter.

"Beautiful, beautiful Kate," he whispered from beside the bed, his fingers just touching hers in midair.

Her eyes turned to sapphire as she saw his body cover hers. From his kiss, she knew that he would demand everything. Now his touch was not gentle, and his hunger fired hers. When she moved under him, it was because she couldn't help herself. He flowed through her senses like music, and she did tremble, as he'd asked, needing him.

His skin was vibrant, many textured, slick under her hands. The male scent of him mixed with the fresh scent of her soap in a combination she found almost painfully erotic.

His touch was knowing, intimate. He took her breast in his mouth, playing with teeth and tongue, one hand holding that breast, the other threading through the soft curls between her legs. Her sigh was almost a sob and he stilled for a moment, trying to hold the hunger. He wanted this to last, but when her legs parted he found another way to please her.

He became drunk with the taste of her, and he

relished the intensity. She felt so good in his arms. His fingers tested the flesh of her hips, lifting her to him. As she called out, he felt a wave of possession so strong he was stunned by it.

*Mine.*

He wanted no one else to have what she had shown him, what she was giving him, no one else to take her so far. She would never want another man but him.

The sound of her voice calling him startled him, and in the next moment he was moving inside her. He folded her legs back, plunging deeply. Her arms reached for him again, and she murmured his name as he took her higher and higher, only to slow and change rhythm.

Hot, sweet passion clouded everything. When he caught sight of the dragon above her bed, that bright image seemed a part of what they shared. He closed his eyes and saw it still.

Kate had long since given up any sense of herself. Her only awareness was of pleasure so sharp it splintered under her skin, in her blood, and she felt a sense of oneness with this man. His flesh and muscle were hers, and his desire. She wondered if he felt it.

He watched her, each response, each flicker of her eyes. He helped her wind her legs around his body. Closing his eyes, he let her set the dance while he moaned softly.

Then she arched and tightened around him, and he responded with slow, strong strokes that filled her completely. Clawing at his arms, she wanted more, the pounding that would take her.

Finally, when he could no longer wait, he changed the pace, wildly taking her farther, farther, until she sobbed in need, then pleasure. With a hoarse cry, he followed, her name in his mind and on his lips.

• • •

Her hand was in his hair. Warm and damp, he was heavy, his weight welcome on her. She felt cleansed, satiated, and so deeply moved by what had happened between them. It was wonderful and terrifying.

She'd known him for a year. She'd read his work, cool and thorough, sometimes angry or determined to find justice. There was also satire or compassion. She'd seen him in the newsroom, coaxing information on the phone, damning dead ends, fighting to make deadline. She'd listened to the jokes he told, the arguments over rights and wrongs. She'd watched him when he was laughing and when he was grim, when he was under pressure and when he was with women.

She'd never known him at all.

Kate was frightened. She'd always believed that things that came too quickly were as quickly gone. Nothing in her life had prepared her for Adam MacHugh.

There had been other men, but Michael had been the first to teach her about infidelity. The lesson had been painful. It had taken every bit of strength she'd built up to leave that behind, to leave behind her the need to prove that she could make him want her alone.

She didn't meet many men she wanted to know in a romantic way. Too often, she had sensed that the risk wasn't worth the fight. There was a rightness she was looking for that she didn't find. So the moments of loneliness came and passed.

Now, at the worst possible time, here was Adam MacHugh. What did he want from her? What did he hope for, and what would he give in exchange?

If she could have kept them from making love so soon she might have, but there had been no choice. Withdrawing from him then would have been more wrong than making love.

He stirred, and she felt the warmth of his breath across her collarbone. Then he seemed to come to himself. "I'm too heavy," he said. He raised himself on his palms at each side of her waist, and fell to her side.

Pulling her close, he let her settle at his shoulder as he stroked her hair. His smile was lazy. "Why do I keep hearing all those clichés in my head? 'It's never been like this before.' Something about 'fireworks' and 'the earth—' "

"Quiet." She silenced him with a kiss, and he felt her shoulders shake with laughter. "You're stepping on my romance."

He did stay quiet after that. He didn't want to put words to the things that were really inside him.

Kate ran her nails lightly over his taut stomach. "You hungry?" It was nearly eleven.

"Starving." He rolled strands of her hair between his fingers.

"Let me go." She brushed her hair over his chest as she pulled away. "I'll see what we've got."

He watched every move as she walked through the bathroom doorway, found the white robe, and pulled it from the floor by the collar. "You do look good, Polanski," he said on a sigh.

She smiled over her shoulder at the compliment and raised her nose high. "*Ms.* Polanski to you, buster." Then she tossed her hair and swayed out to the hall, dragging that robe across the floor like Marilyn with a white mink. His laugh followed her all the way to the kitchen.

Mac went back to the bathroom and put on his pants. He found Kate in the small kitchen, bending down to dig in the refrigerator, and aft was definitely *aft*. The stool at the counter allowed for a terrific view. He took up his position, chin resting on both hands. Kate was too busy talking to herself to notice.

"Hmm, tomatoes . . . Ah, here's one. Green pepper." Her hands relayed the items to the tile counter without disturbing the effect. "Cheddar . . . or Swiss . . . I wonder if he like scallions?"

"He does," Mac answered seriously. At the first sound from behind her, Kate smacked her head on the freezer.

"Ow," she said, turning slowly.

"You're cute when you're clumsy."

"When I'm what?" She glared at him, scallions clutched in a fist at her hip.

"Here." He walked over to her and pried loose the hand that was glued to her forehead. "Let me make it better." When he kissed the bruise, her temple, and along her hairline, she was inclined to lean his way—a little.

"I am not clumsy!" she said to his strong, tanned throat.

"Accident-prone?" he asked, his lips in her hair, one hand rubbing her neck.

"Oh, you . . ." she sputtered, laughing, before she mashed his bare toes with her bare heel.

"Yup." He lifted her so that both of her feet rested on his. "Light on her feet too."

"I'm going to burn your omelette, Adam Mac-Hugh," she said, waving the scallions under his nose.

He winced dramatically, shrugged, and smiled down at her. "Then I'll cook it myself." He took the scallions from her with great care.

"You could?"

His smile widened.

"All right then. I like mine crisp on the outside, tender inside," she said, and dragged herself away. "I'll just have a quick shower." Like a child stealing from the scene of the crime, she ran giggling down the hall.

Kate showered and mopped up a bit of the water on the bathroom floor. Then, wrapped in a towel, she searched through the things in a drawer until she found exactly what was needed.

It was a gown of lavender lace, with a robe in the same shade that wasn't meant to close. It had been a Christmas gift from her mother, one she'd forgotten about until tonight.

She dropped the towel and pulled the gown over her head before turning to the closet mirrors. Oh, it was wonderfully feminine, with skin showing through in all the right places. She remembered how surprised she had been at her mother. But Gina had put on her enigmatic look, nodded, and opened a present of her own.

In the mirrors Kate could see the reflection of the rumpled bed, and she enjoyed the sight before she turned to pull back the spread. Mac would be lovely to sleep with, she thought, so big and warm. One hand reached to the drawer of her bedside table for her brush and she sat on the bed, brushing her hair as she stared dreamily into those long mirrors.

She was glad she hadn't cut her hair. His hands were always in it. Strange, she mused, he was just down the hall, yet she missed him. The brush fell to the bed and she stood quickly, pulling on the lace robe. She moved down the hall so fast that it billowed behind her.

His bare back was to her as he chopped vegetables and sang with the stereo in a pseudo-Otis Redding voice as his hips swung right, then left.

Kate's hand flew to her mouth to stifle her laugh.

He bent his knees, one foot behind the other, and did a low, slick turn. That's when he saw Kate and fell completely out of character.

"Mm-mmm." One hand held a spatula, but the voice was still "Otis." "And I thought you weren't the lace type."

"So now you know you don't know everything."

"Come 'ere and keep me company while I cook." He grinned, then he turned away and poured vegetables on top of the eggs. She took his seat at the counter, watching.

"So far away?" he asked.

"I want to be out of range when that thing blows up." She was referring to the ridiculously grand omelette Mac was tending. He ignored the comment.

"Would you like some wine?" she asked, swiveling back and forth on the stool. "I have an '83 Sauvignon Blanc in the fridge."

"I like."

She got up, walked to the refrigerator, and pulled out the wine. She had to pass Mac to get the corkscrew. Giving in, she planted a quick kiss in the center of his back and went on her way. On the return trip, she saw gooseflesh where the kiss had been and gave him another.

"Sadist," he said, but didn't turn.

She couldn't remember a time she had ever smiled so much.

Mac wouldn't destroy the beauty of his masterpiece, so they ate from the same plate—or rather, platter. Kate didn't have a dining room—Mac said now he knew what to get her for Christmas—and they sat on the living room rug and put the omelette between them on the coffee table. There was candlelight.

"The best omelette you've ever eaten," Mac said, watching her take her first bite. She chewed . . . thoughtfully.

"You had no idea mere eggs could taste like

this," he added. He still hadn't touched his side. He was watching her chew.

"Words cannot describe . . ." He changed tactics. "You hate it."

She swallowed carefully, put down her fork, dabbed her mouth with her napkin, and finally spoke.

"Good."

"Good," he repeated.

"Mm." She nodded. "Good."

"You die!" He reached for her with hands ready to strangle and Kate fell back on the carpet shrieking with laughter.

"It's incredible!" she cried, trying to hold him off. "Ambrosia! The best omelette I've ever tasted—No! Really . . . I swear . . . You stay away from me—Mac!"

# Seven

They slept with limbs entwined, warm skin to warm skin, her leg between his, his hand cradling her breast, her palm over his heart.

Something woke Kate, and she let her gaze wander the room. There was faint light filtering through the blinds.

"What time . . . ?" she murmured.

"It's only six, don't worry." Mac pulled her back down onto the pillows, his hands smoothing her arms. "You were mumbling in your sleep."

A start went through her. "I'm sorry—"

"Don't be," he interrupted her. "I have horrible dreams after late pizza."

She smiled, she had to, shaky or not. "It seems you're turning out to be the most wonderful man."

"That's the plan, Katerina." He kissed her brow.

"What did I say?"

"Nothing I could understand," he reassured her, and began to massage the tenseness from her shoulders. Her eyes closed, and she was sleepy although she'd been wide awake only moments before. His hands were so gentle.

When she woke again, it was to find his arm about her waist, her back to his front. She looked down at the arm encircling her and thought that it might be the arm of an athlete or a sculptor.

Even though he was relaxed in sleep, his muscles were clearly defined just under the skin, which was sprinkled with fine golden red hairs. The hand was wide and long. There were calluses, but not many. The nails were oval and well tended and she badly wanted to kiss the small scratch on one knuckle.

She noticed the light edging around her blinds and arched her neck to try to see the clock from that angle. Suddenly she was aware of Mac's hand moving upward to cup and caress her breast. She held her breath as she felt him stop, felt the shock go through him. Then her breath came out all at once on a laugh as he sat up and tried to clear his head.

"Where am I?" she said, mocking him.

He grinned—it must be admitted—charmingly.

"The best defense is no defense?" she asked, raising a brow.

"The best defense is diversion." He pulled her into his arms for a hug and a tender kiss. "Good morning."

"Impressive tactic." She pushed a strand of tousled blond hair from his brow.

"I was hoping you'd think so." He looked happily into her eyes.

"Do you have time for coffee?" she asked. She knew he didn't have a change of clothes.

"I'd better not. I have an interview to do downtown." He looked at the clock. "I might even make it." One hand was playing with the spaghetti strap of her nightgown. Back and forth over her shoulder, then down to her elbow, forcing the lace over her breast.

Her breath was suddenly shallow, and she watched him bend to take her nipple into his mouth. Her eyes closed.

"Will you have lunch with me?" he asked, his lips brushing back and forth.

"Mm."

"Is that a yes?"

She smiled. "It's an 'mm.' "

He pulled down the other strap, put his mouth to her, and drew hard. "Say yes."

"Ah . . ." She was stalling. She felt the hem of her gown being raised, the heat of his hand on her thigh, then higher. Her heart was pounding.

"Uh-oh," she murmured.

"Say yes, Katie."

". . . Yes."

"I'm going to be late."

"Yes . . ."


It was after ten when she got to her desk. In her hand was an envelope containing the warehouse photographs. She pushed them unseen into her briefcase.

Rob Dunham got off the phone the moment he saw her. He walked across the aisle and leaned on the side of her desk.

"Pappy's looking for you," he said.

"Okay." She continued flipping through her notes. "Thanks, Rob."

"How're things working out with you and Mac?" The question was idle.

Kate glanced up at the man. "Fine," she answered obliquely.

Rob found that very interesting. But he never had a chance to pursue.

"I'd better go see Joe," Kate said, and left Rob there. She had always liked Rob. Hiding behind his homely yet appealing looks and I-see-right-through-you humor was a brilliant writer. He was also a very nice man. But he was Mac's best friend.

Joe met her at the door of his office with a new assignment. Kate gave him a progress report on the Ferranti story. Unfortunately, there wasn't much to tell.

"You and Mac getting along okay?" Joe asked.

"Sure," she said quickly. "So, I'm working on the last of that gas-leakage story this morning, and I'm trying to line up an interview with an old friend of Ferranti's. If I can't get a direct connection, I'm going to storm the Italian's house on the hill." She grinned. "But the guy who runs his interference is built like a truck."

"Sic Mac on him," Joe said with no expression.

She laughed. "It's a thought. Mac's going to talk to Cultural Affairs and see how much pressure they're handling. So far, they seem to be standing behind Ferranti, but I wonder if it's not just saving face."

"Good." Joe leaned back in his chair and gave Kate his serious look. "I'd like to wrap this up. See if you can't find something for me in the next day or two, will you? We may just bury it until the twenty-third and make it a two-part, the finish on the twenty-fourth when the exhibit appears or not."

Kate saluted and went to the door.

"Oh, Kate." She turned and Joe looked her up and down. "You look very pretty today."

She blushed furiously, then laughed. "Thanks, Joe."

Kate had a hundred calls to make. On the way in that morning she had run by Ferranti's warehouse and found electronic locks on the doors. What she wanted now was a talk with Jarré.

"Detective Jarré speaking," he answered his phone. His voice was cultured, the accent French.

"Detective Jarré, this is Kate Polanski with the *L.A. Daily.* I wonder if I might make an appointment with you for an interview." She made her tone more personal than businesslike.

"An interview?"

"Yes. Perhaps we could meet for drinks when you go off duty. At Trumps?" He would know that Trumps was not the usual haunt for a reporter. It was palm trees, and blond-hostess pretentious. It might be enough bait.

"Why would you wish to interview me, Miss Polanski?" He sounded as if the idea amused him.

She'd have to give him more. "I'm told that you were acquainted with Riccardo Ferranti in Paris some years ago."

"Yes." The voice was not quite so lazy now.

For a moment Kate thought she had lost him, then he said abruptly, "At Trumps then? Seven o'clock?"

"Seven is fine, Detective."

The line went dead and Kate was left holding the receiver. "Hmm."

For the next two hours she worked on the follow-up story about gas leakage in the Fairfax area and the residents' recovery, sandwiching in calls to local merchants for direct quotes. She was just tagging the story when she felt someone kiss the back of her neck, then nuzzle her ear.

She couldn't believe it, and for a moment she couldn't even speak. She turned her head and saw Mac standing there grinning at her. She looked around the news room. No one was watching them, which probably meant that no one had missed that kiss. Rob's face was three inches from his computer screen, his shoulders hunched. The assistant city editor had his chair turned away—away from Kate and Mac, and away from his own desk.

Kate was furious, more than furious.

"Could I speak to you downstairs, Mac?" she asked. Controlling her voice was an effort. She opened her bottom desk drawer, grabbed her purse, slammed the drawer shut, and stood stiffly.

"Oh, I think that could be arranged," Mac said. He put his arm through hers and began to march down the aisle to the elevators. "How about Thai food, or would you rather have something else?" The elevator arrived, and Kate stepped in and pressed "B."

"We're going to the pressroom?" Mac asked her.

She stared at the lighted numbers and gave a nod. It was beginning to occur to Mac that something was wrong. The elevator stopped, the doors opened, and the sound of machinery filled the air. Kate waved to a technician she knew, then walked on between the giant presses until she and Mac were completely alone. Then she turned on her heel to face him.

"How could you!" she shouted over the noise of the presses. "How could you do that in front of the whole city room!" She wanted to throw something. "It never even occurred to me that I would have to ask that you keep what is between us private." She crossed her arms tightly, one over the other. "You couldn't wait, could you? You had to show everybody the new conquest!"

"It wasn't like that!"

"Oh, no? What was it like?" Her hair was coming loose, her eyes were brilliant, and her color was high. She knew she was saying things she didn't mean, but she couldn't stop.

"I was happy to see you," Mac said, also shouting to be heard, "I wanted to touch you. I don't see what's so horrible about that!"

The look in her eyes pinned him. "Then you don't know your reputation!"

"Are you saying you're ashamed to be with me?"

Now Mac was getting angry. He was such a bad guy?

"*Be* with you! I've only *been* with you a day and a night!"

"Two days!" This was going all wrong, he thought. He wanted to hold her, tell her how much he had missed her. He turned away a moment, running one hand through his hair. Then the air left his lungs in a powerful sigh. "Kate." His tone was different now.

"What?" she asked suspiciously.

"I didn't think." His eyes met hers. "I'm sorry."

"You . . . are?"

"Mm."

Stepping closer, she lifted her mouth to his ear. "Is that a 'yes'?"

He took her by the arms. "That's an 'mm.' "

Her hands encircled his neck. "Say yes."

His kiss answered her.


They went to Mac's Thai place for lunch and Kate made him explain all the dishes. He was so serious about it that she didn't remember anything he said. But she remembered every expression that crossed his face.

They held hands and touched knees under the table.

"You make that appointment this morning?" she asked.

"I got the interview." His grin was cocky.

"O-o-oh," she teased him.

After the waitress had taken their order Mac ran his thumb over her knuckles and asked, "How's our story going?"

Kate shrugged indifferently. "Well, how much could happen in a couple of hours?"

"Kate." He made the word two syllables.

She dropped the pose and rested her chin on one hand. "I stopped by the warehouse this morning and it's already secured by an electronic system. That means Ferranti had people working on it as soon as Sunday or Sunday night."

"You didn't break in to check for the shipment?"

Kate thought his expression a bit smug. She waited until the appetizer was placed between them and she had reached for a skewer. "I don't know enough about electronics." When she saw his smile she kept her tone matter-of-fact. "Of course, I could give Uncle Tony a call."

Mac knew he was being taken. He finished chewing, swallowed, and fixed Kate with a look of steel. "Yesterday, in a moment—his *single* moment—of good humor, your uncle told me he was a locksmith."

"He is." She licked sauce from the tip of her thumb.

"Hit me."

She raised both brows.

"Explain," he translated.

"My aunt Maria died in Italy when Pietro was born. Angelo was only two. That's when Uncle Tony moved to America. He asked Mama to come along to take care of the boys. At first he worked as a locksmith, but he was an expert with any kind of locking device. He took some classes, expanded little by little, changed his ad in the Yellow Pages"—she smiled—"and what a celebration *that* was. Now he owns a modest home-security business."

"What's it called?" Mac was hoping he hadn't heard of it.

"Ace Securities." Kate laughed and held her napkin over her mouth. "He wanted to be first in the book."

Mac had to smile. She was as entertaining as

the story. He had seen the home-style commercial Ace ran on television, but still he pressed just a little harder.

"What makes you think *Uncle Tony* would know a system an Italian specialist would use?"

Kate grinned. "He keeps up."

Mac made a face and gave her a long look. "How's the food?"

"Sometimes, MacHugh, you're more Italian than I am."

She waited until the entrées were served before getting back to Ferranti. "Benjamin Friedman," she said, stabbing a bite of meat. "That's the listed owner of the warehouse. But I don't think he's important. The library didn't have anything on him, he hasn't got a record. You ever hear of Ben Friedman?"

Mac shook his head. "Cultural Affairs now says Ferranti is legally authorized to take whatever steps he feels necessary to protect the exhibit. They say they have complete confidence in him." Mac gave her his ironic look. "But the words were spoken in a shaky voice."

"So. Then there's Jarré. Mm, this is great, Mac. You knew who Jarré was when you saw him at the warehouse, didn't you?"

"I knew he was a cop. I did a story on a case of his last year. Break-ins on Rodeo."

"He's meeting me at Trumps later this evening." She took a sip of the sweet iced coffee. "I'll see what I can get out of him about Ferranti."

"How late?" Mac asked casually.

She smiled. He wasn't a very good actor. "We should be finished by nine. Why? Interested in the results?"

"No." He took a bite from her plate. "I'm interested in sleeping with you tonight."

She'd been set up, but for his sake she pre-

"alluring"... "inspiring"...
"irresistible"...

# Loveswept

## EXAMINE 4 LOVESWEPT NOVELS FOR
# 15 Days FREE!

Turn page for details

# America's most popular, most compelling romance novels...

# Loveswept

Here, at last...love stories that really involve you! Fresh, finely crafted novels with story lines so believable you'll feel you're actually living them!

Read a Loveswept novel and you'll experience all the very real feelings of two people as they discover and build an involved relationship: laughing, crying, learning and loving. Characters you can relate to... exciting places to visit...unexpected plot twists...all in all, exciting romances that satisfy your mind and delight your heart.

And now you can be sure you'll never, ever miss a single Loveswept title by enrolling in our special reader's home delivery service. A service that will bring all four new Loveswept romances published every month into your home—and deliver them to you *before* they appear in the bookstores!

---

## Examine 4 Loveswept Novels for

# 15 Days FREE!

To introduce you to this fabulous service, you'll get four brand-new Loveswept releases not yet in the bookstores. These four exciting new titles are yours to examine for 15 days without obligation to buy. Keep them if you wish for just $9.95 plus postage and handling and any applicable sales tax.

SEND NO MONEY NOW.
RETURN THIS
POSTAGE-PAID CARD TODAY!

tended to be shocked. "You can meet me by the pool at nine-thirty. It's warm tonight. Of course, you'll have to jump the fence." Her lashes swept down over her blue eyes. "It's not really very high."

His smile acknowledged the challenge.

Back at the paper, Mac behaved in a way that was perfectly discreet and terribly respectful. So much so, in fact, that Kate had to pinch him when she found him in the editorial library late in the afternoon.

At four-thirty, she passed his desk, dropping a crumpled note in his lap. He was on the phone, but he caught the ball of paper in the other hand by reflex. Kate walked on to the elevator.

"Hold a second, will you?" he said into the phone. He didn't wait for an answer, but set the receiver over his shoulder as he opened the note, his gaze on Kate. He glanced down. It held only three words, but his smile was wide as he looked up to see the elevator doors closing in front of her. She gave a little wave and mouthed the words on the note.

"Don't be late."

"The lady's got style," he murmured, and shook his head. Then he remembered the phone. "Okay, Mrs. Turner. You said you have some information for me?"

Kate had given herself plenty of time. She *dressed:* thin white linen trousers and a camisole, with a loose jacket in a salmon color so light it was almost white, and high-heeled sandals. She arrived at Trumps at five to seven, and saw Jarré in the lounge, sitting on a small couch next to a potted palm. He wore a gray shirt and pants, European design. He had dark hair and eyes, and

Kate guessed him to be in his midthirties. Again she thought he had the look of a cat. He stood as she approached him.

"You are Mademoiselle Polanski?" he asked.

"Detective Jarré?" she returned with a smile, and held out her hand.

He took her hand in his. "You are not the usual reporter." He gestured her to the chair opposite him, on the other side of a low table.

"I intend to take that as a compliment, Detective." Kate was aware of the shrewd assessment in his eyes as she took her notebook from her purse and placed it in her lap.

"But of course." He inclined his head. There was a half bottle of wine in an ice bucket next to the table, and an empty glass in front of her. "Wine?" he asked. " Or would you care for something else?"

"Wine, please."

He poured, then touched her glass with his. "*A votre santé.*" He took one sip, and set down the glass. "Now, Mademoiselle, how may I help you?"

Kate chose the direct approach. "I'd like you to tell me what you know about Riccardo Ferranti, what you think of his actions in connection with the Chinese exhibit."

He studied her quite openly for a few seconds. Kate waited. Then he reached again for his glass. "When I was nineteen, Riccardo hired me to run errands for his company. That job paid for my schooling, and later I worked in both his Paris and London offices until I married an American and moved here ten years ago."

"So you know him very well?" Kate was annoyed to feel a twinge of jealousy.

"Riccardo is a good man. He is also an expert at his work." Jarré's expression changed then. Something flickered in his eyes, and was as quickly gone. "He will make whatever provisions necessary to protect the exhibit."

"Do you think there was sufficient reason for the exhibit to be taken from the museum to be protected?"

"Yes."

The answer had come quick and sure. "Such as . . . ?"

"Ah, my dear Mademoiselle Polanski, my response to that question would have to be off-the-record."

She grinned. "Call me Kate."

"Guy," he responded.

"So." She looked down, trying to conceal her eagerness. "Guy, what do you mean when you say 'off the record'?"

"I mean strictly off the record because I could be fired for telling you."

She nodded. "And if I only use the information after confirming with another source?"

"You can use it. Just do not quote me."

There was a puzzle here, Kate thought. Jarré was curiously relaxed. But she would have to put that aside in favor of another puzzle. "What happened that made Riccardo Ferranti remove the exhibit from the museum?"

Guy sipped his wine slowly. Kate had the impression this man was slow and careful in most things. "A necklace was stolen."

She raised her brows. This was a surprise indeed. "But it wasn't reported; at least the wire services haven't picked it up."

"No, the museum wants to give Riccardo a chance at recovery. They'll wait until the twenty-fourth." His mouth lifted in a half smile. "I imagine they're using the time to think up ways to approach the Chinese with the bad news."

"What kind of necklace?"

"A silver heirloom necklace from one of the ethnic minority groups of central China."

"How valuable is it?" Kate wondered why someone would steal a necklace made of silver.

Guy smiled. "This necklace is from the Flowery Miao people, handed down in one family for generations. It is made in collar tiers with dangling figures in silver, covering the torso from neck to waist. Some of the ornaments are believed to be nearly a thousand years old." He poured them each more wine. "The women of the Miao would rather die than sell such a necklace. This particular piece was found with the body of a dead mountain trader in 1950. It was almost certainly stolen from the original owners. And"—he looked out—"it is priceless."

Kate was suitably impressed. "When was it taken from the museum?"

"On the day it arrived."

"But how?"

"There was a small reception to celebrate the arrival." He pulled out a pack of Gitanes, and offered her one. Kate declined. "Then, sometime between nine and eleven, the storage space was broken into, the necklace stolen." He lit the cigarette with a gold lighter.

"Do you think it was someone on that guest list?"

"It's possible." He was noncommittal.

"Was the job amateur or professional?"

"That is something you would have to ask Riccardo." He blew a lungful of smoke into the air and looked down the aisle.

Kate didn't understand why he would take her so far and then back away. She drew a deep breath. "I would like to do just that. Can you arrange it for me?"

Guy looked at her with a kind of amused awe,

then his smile widened to show small, even white teeth. He leaned back against the couch, crossed his arms, and cocked his head at another angle. "I don't know. Perhaps. It might be interesting to see how Riccardo responds to your questions."

Now it was Kate's turn to be amused. Just what was up this man's sleeve? And what kind of relationship did he have with Riccardo Ferranti?

Guy looked at the burning tip of his cigarette, then put it to his lips and exhaled the blue smoke once more before he spoke again. "You can be reached at your paper?"

Kate picked up her purse, took out a card, and scribbled on the back. "This is my home number."

He took the card from her, and now the speculation in his eyes was of the male variety. Kate responded by changing to a strictly businesslike manner.

"What will Ferranti do?" she asked.

Guy shrugged in the way particular to the French. "He will try to find the necklace and guard the rest of the exhibit."

"You're helping him?"

That strange look again, then Guy nodded once. "Of course."

Kate was puzzled. She sensed some conflict there, but perhaps it was just her imagination. It might be as simple as a disagreement between the two men on how things should be handled. But it could be mistrust. Did Jarré think Ferranti had faked the theft? She wanted to ask why he had stopped working for Ferranti, but the man before her had withdrawn so much that she decided to wait for another time. She raised her glass.

"Are you still married, Guy?" she asked.

"Yes, my wife runs a boutique on Beverly Drive. Sometimes I am convinced that it is the difference in our schedules that keeps us content with each other."

Kate smiled, as he had intended her to do.

By the time she left the restaurant, it was dark out, and the drive home seemed endless. At a stoplight she removed her jacket. It was a perfect night for a swim, she thought, warm with a bit of a breeze, bright with the light of a thousand stars. And she was early. It was ridiculous that just turning her corner would make her feel breathless.

Though she usually entered her house by the front gate because of the mailbox, tonight she went to the back so that she could turn on the lights for Mac. Looking up at the ten-foot brick wall, she grinned and wondered if he'd really try. Her key was in the lock when she heard the sounds. As she pushed the gate open she could swear she heard music.

She stepped forward and her gaze swung left, then right. There were Japanese lanterns hung in the yard and a picnic basket on one of the lounges. A portable cassette recorder was playing Frank Sinatra while someone was doing laps in her pool.

Kate looked around again. This romance from Adam MacHugh?

Mac swam to the side of the pool and braced himself on the edge with his forearms. "Do you know what you look like with that streetlight shining down on you?" he asked.

She smiled and shook her head as she walked closer.

"Beautiful, Polanski." She was near enough that he could reach out and touch her if he tried. "Just beautiful."

"Are you coming out?" she asked, smiling.

"Come in." He waited to see if she would.

Kate stood there a moment, then without another word, she turned, walked to the outside corner of the house, opened a grate, and pushed a switch. The pool became lit with shades of blue and yellow, every ripple a different color. Her shoes clicked against the pavement as she returned to the lounge and dropped her purse, briefcase, jacket, and earrings. The rest of her clothes followed. She walked to the low diving board and dove into the water.

It was as warm as bathwater, silk against the skin. When she surfaced, Mac was there, his eyes wide and dark. He raised his arms, and she moved into them to kiss those eyes, one after the other. The lashes were wet and spiky, his skin warm to the touch. His mouth, when it met hers, had a different kind of heat.

His arms wrapped around her. He held her against the length of his body as they kissed again and again. She felt the strength in that body, in his arms and thighs. In the muscled chest that pressed against her breasts. She could feel his desire for her through his trunks, and in the hands that caressed her. Finally, he drew back.

"Hello," he said.

"Hello," she whispered, then looked about in surprise. "You kept us afloat."

He smiled. "Oh, underwater's good too." She hardly had time for a breath before he dragged her back for another kiss and let them slip under.

Kate let that kiss go on until Mac pushed off the bottom and the two of them splashed through the surface, gasping for air and laughing wildly.

"What's in the basket?" she asked, swimming backward, away from him.

He breaststroked after her. "A few odds and ends."

She eyed him suspiciously. "You weren't one of those public-pool bullies whom swam around dunking everyone smaller than he, were you?"

His face showed outrage at the thought, but he was coming closer until . . . Kate dunked him first and swam like mad for the ladder. He splashed after her, making horrible noises, but let her get away so that he could watch her run for a towel.

"Tough guy," she said. She stuck her nose in the air as she dragged the giant towel around her. The air was chilly after the warmth of the pool. "You'd better come out. I'm going to raid that basket without you."

"There's no lock." He grinned at her before he levered himself up and out of the pool. "I remembered you've a habit of breaking and entering."

"Clever man," she said fondly, flipping open one side of the basket. Then she laughed out loud. She was staring at a bucket of Kentucky Fried-Chicken and a six pack of Japanese beer.

Mac.

She turned to find him behind her. Her chin rose and her eyes sparkled. "My kind of party."

# *Eight*

"Did you climb my wall?" Kate asked. She was sitting on the edge of the diving board, one foot swinging, while Mac was treading water below.

"What do you think?" His fingers circled one slender ankle, then slipped away.

"I would say . . ." She looked over her shoulder to the brick wall. "You climbed the front gate. The iron curls would make it easy. Then you came to the back gate, opened it from the inside, and unloaded the car. What I don't understand is why you weren't arrested."

Mac remembered the climb. He was rather pleased with himself. "Tell me what happened tonight."

"Jarré is a strange man, Mac." Her foot swung back and forth, her toes almost skimming the water. "He told me what he wanted me to know, then nothing more. I was given confidential information quite deliberately. And there's something going on between Jarré and Ferranti. At least from Jarré's side. I can't tell if it's jealousy or competition, or if he really doesn't trust the man. He says all the right things, but . . . there's a look in his eye whenever he talks about Ferranti." She bit her lip, then looked down at Mac. "It's not love."

Mac swam to the ladder and caught the towel she tossed him. "Come on, let's go in," he said, quickly scrubbing at his arms and chest. "It's getting cold out here."

"I think he's going to arrange for me to meet Ferranti," she said as she gathered their clothes and the basket. "I'll take this in, you blow out the lanterns."

Mac grunted assent, blew out the candles, and met Kate at the back door. He followed her through the laundry room to the kitchen, where they put away the rest of the food and beer. Then, his arm around her shoulders, he led her to the master bathroom, snagged her towel off her, and pushed her into the shower. It was all very domestic and routine.

It was marvelous.

Kate soaped the loofah and scrubbed his back while he stretched like a cat. "Why aren't you asking me what he said?" she demanded as she worked on his shoulders.

"You'll tell me or you won't." His shoulders rose and fell beneath her hands. "Besides . . ." He turned his face to profile. "I can always beat it out of you." He anticipated the blow from the sponge and ducked, then spun around to grab her wrists and yank her to him. The kiss that followed was little more than a smack, but the next was very satisfactory.

"So," he said, holding her against him as he soaped up and down her spine. "Tell me."

She drew away slightly to look into his eyes. "I never imagined sharing an off-the-record statement with another reporter, Mac. I'm not sure it's a good idea."

"Katie, believe it or not, I have principles too." His hands came up to cup her shoulders. "But we've got to start working together. I'm not going to print or repeat anything said to you off the record, but I need to have the same information you have."

Kate felt a twinge at that; she knew she hadn't been fair. She couldn't be completely open, not just yet, but she could give him this. So, as quickly as possible, she relayed to Mac everything Jarré had told her.

"I know a secretary at the museum," Mac said when she was finished. "Let me see if I can get a copy of that guest list." He was staring at the tile in front of him. Then he shook his head. "Why didn't Jarré continue to work for Ferranti in America?" He poured shampoo into his hand and started washing Kate's hair as he mused aloud. "Why would he become a cop when he could make more money in free-lance security? Suppose he learned Ferranti hadn't reformed after all?"

"I don't know." She tilted her head back to rinse her hair. "But I do know he wouldn't have told me tonight. I'm going to badger him tomorrow about that meeting with Ferranti. Maybe I can find out something then." She pushed open the shower door and went straight for the warming rod that held fresh towels. "Ferranti's been able to avoid reporters so far, but I could see that Jarré liked the idea of me getting to his old buddy to put the screws to him." She handed a towel to Mac and smiled at his tan line. "What do you do to get a tan like that?"

"Racquetball, some sailing." He ruffled his hair with the towel. "You like sailing?"

"We'll have to find out." She twisted a towel around her hair and tucked it into place. He held her terry robe for her to slip on.

Standing behind her, he looked into the mirror and saw them together. Kate met his eyes in the mirror. Her skin was dew-moist, lips full and slightly parted, her eyes a deep shattering blue. The robe was unbelted, allowing glimpses of skin that seduced with every movement.

Mac felt his body's instant response and his eyes became dark. His hair was shining wet, and the hair on his chest was still in damp whirls. His color was bronze in contrast to the white of her robe.

For a long moment they stood motionless, staring into each other's eyes. Then Mac's hands came around her to rest on her collarbone. He felt the great breath she took, the hammering of her heart, and he ran the tips of his fingers slowly, slowly down her skin inside the lapels of the robe until he reached the swell of her breasts. Her face was flushed now, her lips a dark rose.

He pushed closer until his body was comforted by the heat of hers, then he let his fingers glide in a feather touch to the tips of her breasts. But he wouldn't spread his hands to hold her; he only gave wisps of sensation. His fingers slid over her ribs to find her navel, then traveled back up.

Kate arched backward to feel his strength, his need for her. His hands moved down again, over the soft skin of her belly, still in tantalizing circles, through the blond curls. Her arms rose to clasp his neck behind her, her head bent to the side.

His throat tightened. There was such sweetness in her, the way she opened to him, gave to him. He let each stroke linger and melt into another, inviting her deeper and deeper into the sensuality, and when her face changed there was a subtle difference in his caress.

Here was love, he thought, and she was beautiful. He would give as much as she could take.

Kate knew she had become someone else because of him, someone wild and free. She had become someone who could bend, who was no longer brittle and alone, and she knew it every time he touched her.

She turned, her mouth searching for his. He kissed her, his tongue thrusting, hungry. Then she shuddered against him and moaned into his mouth. She twisted around and held him tightly to her, every muscle straining, lungs needing more oxygen than she would allow.

"Katie," he whispered into her hair. He kissed her ear, his tongue exploring each curve and hollow. She shivered in his arms, and he backed her to the sink and lifted her. He didn't want to scare her, but he was losing control and couldn't hold on much longer. "I've got to . . . Oh, Katie love, I've got to have you."

Her arms tightened, and her legs came around him. Her head fell back as she took him into her. His hands stroked her thighs and back, her breasts, then he held her hips and thrust deeply, his breathing ragged, hurried. Her body responded to each movement of his, each caress, his excitement feeding hers. His arms lifted her and she knew a woman's power. He was lost to passion, and nothing could have aroused her more. His eyes closed, his skin darkly flushed, he was vulnerable and powerful, harsh and gentle. His breathing was loud in her ears, and blood raced through her veins, every nerve electric. With a raw sound, his mouth found hers.

"Kate, we're lying on the bathroom floor." Mac's gaze was fixed on the towel rack to his left.

"Your mind's a blank," she answered playfully.

"I can't believe I took you here, like that."

She blinked and rubbed one hip thoughtfully. "I think I have rug burn."

"Ah, Katie." He laughed and hugged her close. "I'm sorry."

Her fingers twined in his hair. "Don't be sorry." She kissed a cheekbone, his jaw, his soft mouth. "I couldn't be." She kissed his throat and rested there.

"You have some lotion we can put on it?" His fingers combed through her damp hair, and he loved the way it clung to him.

"Lotion?" she asked drowsily. She could sleep for days.

Mac looked down at her and smiled, then stood, pulling her up in his arms.

"I love it when you carry me," she murmured. "No one ever carried me before. No one ever touched me the way you do."

He let her slide down to lean against him while he turned back the spread. When that was done, he laid her on the bed and covered her with the sheet.

"Don't go 'way," she said to the pillow.

"I'll just be a second, honey," he said softly.

*Honey.* She liked the sound of that. She smiled as she turned on her stomach and switched direction on the pillow. She wanted to see him when he came back. But her eyelids were so heavy.

There came the sliding sound of the sheet, then his weight on the bed beside her. She felt the caress of the oil he had warmed with both hands.

"Umm. So nice." She snuggled down farther as his hands massaged gently.

Taking care of Kate felt more right than anything Mac could remember. She was so small under his hands, so trusting. He lifted her fragrant hair from her neck and let his fingers work her muscles. Then he smiled at her sudden frown of concentration.

"Mac?" Her delicate brows drew down.

"Yes, Kate."

"Don't let me fall in love, will you? Don't let me . . ." Her voice was trailing off. "Not yet . . ."

His hands continued to run lightly over her skin for a few minutes until he was certain she was asleep. His expression was preoccupied when he bent to kiss the soft skin of her neck.

A phone was ringing much too loudly. Kate's hand was lead-heavy as she lifted it to stop the noise. She mumbled incoherently, and put the phone to her ear.

"Kate?"

Her eyes flew open, she went immediately to *alert*. "Guy." She drew the sheet around her and pulled herself up to a sitting position. Her hair covered half her face and she glanced at the clock. Not quite eight o'clock.

"I believe," Guy said, "I may have a way for you to meet Riccardo, if you still wish it."

"You talked him into meeting with me?" She was understandably surprised. Ferranti had avoided reporters since the exhibit's arrival. When necessary, he had used the chauffeur to dissuade the more persistent ones.

"I have arranged for you to have an invitation to the Warwick party in Bel Air. But once inside, you will have to manage your own introduction. I wish to enjoy the fire, but not the heat. *Tu comprends, Kate?*" She heard the smile in his voice. The man did have a certain charm.

She tossed back her hair and smiled in return. "I believe I do, *mon capitain*. Perhaps I can even arrange to be introduced to Detective Jarré?"

There was a bark of laughter over the line. "*Très bien, chérie. Et maintenant,* the invitation is for this evening after eight. It will be delivered by messenger to your newspaper before noon. It would be politic to bring an escort." He made the statement sound like a question.

"After eight," she confirmed. It would have to be Mac, she thought.

"Ciao, Kate."

"Good-bye," she answered automatically, and held the receiver long after the dial tone. There was so much under the surface of any conversation with this man. It was frustrating, and tantalizing.

She replaced the phone, then looked around and suddenly realized she was quite alone. Where was *he*?

Throwing back the covers, she picked up the robe Mac had placed at the foot of her bed. He wasn't in the bathroom, though his shaving kit was. She found him pouring coffee in the kitchen, clean-shaven, neatly dressed.

"Now I've missed coffee in bed," she said, thrusting out her bottom lip.

He turned and leaned back on the counter behind him, wondering if he would ever get used to the sight of her. She had brushed her hair and it lay in waves over one shoulder like dark honey with bits of sun. Her skin glowed. Her smile was sleepy and quite beautiful.

"It feels like a hundred years," he said, and held out his arms.

She walked into them. "It's so good to have you to wake up to," she whispered, her cheek upon his chest. Her head fell back. "And you say the most wonderful things."

She was lifted almost off her feet as his arms tightened and he kissed her. Then he hugged her, rocking, his forehead on her shoulder.

"Good sleep?" He bit her neck lightly.

"Great." She pulled back slightly. "Were you there?"

He smiled. "Somewhere there."

"I just got a call from Guy Jarré."

He felt her body tense with excitement. "And?"

"You busy tonight?"


It was six P.M. and Kate was alone in her house. She set her coffee and leather briefcase on the kitchen table, and released the side locks on the case. Inside was a manila envelope. She took it out and sat down at the table. She had asked for eight-by-tens of the warehouse pictures. Lifting the flap, she pulled out the first photograph. She stared at it for a moment, then placed it on the far corner of the table. She reached for the second, the third, the fourth, until they all lay before her.

Her heart was beating in her ears; her breath came quick and light. She lifted a hand and held it over one of the photographs for the longest time. Then she gathered up all the pictures, thrust them back into the envelope, and pushed that beneath the other papers in her case.

It was time to dress.


The lights below his house on the ridge shimmered in jewel colors under the black sky. The air was damp, with a warm breeze that brushed his face in a careless touch.

Riccardo Ferranti felt a melancholy he had not allowed himself for many years. He was tiring of this round of parties and society chatter, evening clothes and flirtation. He longed to be at sea, the wheel under his hands, the wind clean and sharp.

He turned from the weathered wooden railing.

The Warwick family had invited him to another of these parties, and although he didn't want to, he would go because it was important that he remain visible. There were suspicions enough without people thinking he had disappeared.

"Riccardo?" The man who called for him was his protector, his friend for twenty-five years.

"I come, Andrew." Riccardo looked at the battered boxer's face and wondered if the problems with this job might not be too much this time. Whatever touched him, touched Andrew. They were rarely apart.

Riccardo wanted to get this business over with and return to his yacht. Perhaps he would go to Greece. In Greece the sun would bake away this emptiness.

Ah, you show the age, Riccardo, he thought as he followed Andrew to the car. Fifty-five. Soon he would be an old man, dreaming of love lost. Next, it would be eighteen-year-old girls. A dry smile tightened his lips as he bent to step into the backseat of the dark Mercedes.

The Art Deco white of the Warwick house was startling to the eye. The entry hall floor was set with large black and white marble tiles in a chessboard design. The hall opened onto another room of white, which in turn led to the white and green ballroom.

Julia Warwick was the first to greet Riccardo. She was an attractive woman in her forties, secure in her money and position. Though her perfume was expensive, there was too much of it. Her hair was an improbable red and her jewelry clanked like armor. Riccardo liked her anyway.

"Riccardo." She held out her hands to him. "I am *so* glad you could come. Let's find you a drink." She pulled him along, slipping one hand through his arm and tilting her head conspiratorially.

"*Someone* told me that we're going to have a giant treasure hunt for your exhibit at the end of the month."

"My dear Julia, I have to tell you that this story is quite untrue." He scanned the crowd and saw Guy's wife, Sydney, laughing with a wealthy Argentine man Riccardo knew. Guy would be somewhere close by. He smiled indulgently at Julia and finished sotto voce, "I am afraid the Chinese officials have no sense of humor."

An hour later Riccardo was standing in the archway to the ballroom, wishing he were anywhere else, when a young woman caught his eye. She was so much like a memory he had brushed away, he could not turn his gaze from her.

Her profile was to him, and her features were Florentine cameo; straight nose, full lips, rounded chin. Her hair was antique gold, drawn up to reveal the delicate line of her throat. She was watching the dancers on the floor, commenting every so often to the tall blond man standing next to her.

As Riccardo took a step forward for a better view, she shrugged and turned toward him. That shrug, her stance, were so mockingly familiar. He frowned, then dismissed the notion.

Now he could see her full face. The dress she wore was a bright cerise, clinging, strapless, and utterly simple. French, he thought. Her shoulders were a lovely cream above the bandeau bodice. Riccardo smiled, admiring her style. He lifted his drink, silently toasting her beauty, then saw the sparkle of diamond from her necklace. His hand clenched about the glass and his face tightened in shock. His gaze followed the line of gold chain to the pearl suspended from it. It was an unusual piece, a baroque pearl, bluish in tint, an inch and a half long. It was surrounded by a golden mermaid, held on one side by her hair, low on the other side by her tail. Small diamonds glittered wetly in her hair and on the tail.

The glass never met his lips. He handed it blindly to someone passing him and moved to her through the crowd of dancers. Nothing on earth could have stopped him.

Standing in the middle of this mélange of celebrities, professionals, and society-professionals, Mac had a chance to take a good look at himself. It gave him quite a jolt.

He was a reporter, not a cop or a champion. Yet here he was again, bodyguard for Kate. Why did he do it? Why had he let her handle the only two real leads they had, Ferranti and Jarré? If he'd worked with any other reporter, he would have gone his own way by now, attacked this story head-on, not from the mystery angle. This wasn't reporting, it was playing Hammett.

Kate was beautiful, very important to him, and their relationship had hit him like a flash fire. But Mac had just realized he had put something of himself aside for her, and he didn't like it. Kate had been right. This was her story, she had made sure of that. He only hoped, for both their sakes, that it hadn't been deliberate.

She turned to him now. "I think Signor Ferranti is about to pay us a visit," she said.

A look had come over her face that surprised Mac. It was almost a . . . joyful fear. Then he saw a man's tanned hand on her bare arm, turning her toward the elegant gray-haired figure. The bearded man seemed stunned as he stared at Kate.

Mac didn't understand. This had the feel of a confrontation, but the two were strangers. He sensed Kate's excitement at the meeting. It was in her posture, the stillness of her face.

*"Signorina,"* Riccardo said, letting his gaze wander over her, watching for familiar expressions. "Would you do me the honor?" The words were stiff, but his eyes were compelling. There was no other possible answer. She put her hand in his.

Mac was left standing alone, his mouth open, ready to speak. Cold, dark anger rushed through him. He had known Kate had a personal interest in this story. But she had certainly lied to him—probably from the beginning—by omission.

"You are Gianetti's daughter," Riccardo said to Kate as they danced. His steps were smooth, much practiced.

"How did you know?" she asked.

"Just so beautiful was your mother," he said. "But I saw what you meant me to see; the pearl I had designed for Gianetta as a wedding gift so long ago. I could not wait for our wedding. I gave it to her the night of her nineteenth birthday."

Kate stared into Riccardo's chocolate-colored eyes. "I've always wondered about the color of your eyes." Her voice was husky, her hands unsteady.

"She is living?" His urgency could not be disguised.

Kate nodded solemnly.

"Married?" It was an effort to appear casual.

"No," Kate said shortly, her eyes down to hide her expression. "She doesn't know I've found you." She bit her lip. "She doesn't read the paper."

"That is better, until my business is settled." Then the warm brown eyes softened. "What is your name?"

It took her a moment to say it. "Katerina."

He looked at her as if she had given him a great gift, and his step slowed. "My daughter." He was certain for the first time. He examined her every feature. Her eyes were the blue of the Mediterranean, her mouth sweetly curved. "It was the name of my mother. I knew you were Gia's child, but . . ."

Kate looked straight at him. "She told me all she knew about you. She's never forgotten."

He looked blindly over her shoulder, his jaw tightly clenched, his mind a lifetime away. Then he saw Guy watching them from the ballroom entrance. Their eyes met; they nodded. Riccardo looked back down at the young woman in his arms. "We must find somewhere to talk in private. Can you meet me later tonight?" He glanced at his watch. "At twelve o'clock in the bar of the Beverly Wilshire?"

"Yes," Kate said immediately. "But you have to know, I am a reporter."

He smiled. He was a man of great presence, and even Kate was aware of the pull of his charm. When he spoke, his eyes were gentle and . . . almost proud. "Then we will have to make the story a good one."

As he escorted her back to Mac, she said hurriedly, "I think you had better call me Kate. It's Kate Polanski. The man I'm with is also a reporter, my partner."

Her father gave her a curious look, but said nothing.

Mac looked very handsome in his dinner jacket, but as they got closer, Kate could see the tightness about his mouth that signified trouble. She had no idea that the impression she was giving Mac was that she was involved with Riccardo in a very personal way. All the time they had been dancing, she and Riccardo had hardly looked away from each other.

"Adam MacHugh," she said when they stood before him, "I'd like you to meet Signor Riccardo Ferranti."

The men shook hands, and Kate noticed a dangerous glint in Mac's eyes. Trying to avoid trouble, she held out her own hand to Riccardo. "Well, Signor Ferranti," she said lightly, "thank you very much for your cooperation. I'm looking forward to our interview." Their eyes met, a message passed.

Riccardo acknowledged his cue and bowed. "My pleasure, signorina." Then he added with his eyes half-closed and a whisper of a smile, "You are a most graceful dancer." With that, he nodded once in Mac's direction and walked away.

Kate couldn't help but let her gaze follow him. *Her father.* Italian children said "Papa." She wondered if she could ever call that slim, sophisticated man "Papa." She swallowed and blinked quickly.

Had she done the right thing? Would it have been better to let the past lie, as her uncle Tony was so fond of saying? Would this only hurt her mother? And what if her father was still a thief?

"I've had about enough," a low, angry voice said from behind her.

Her head whipped around. Whatever was the matter with Mac?

"Are you ready to go?" He gripped her elbow so tightly that she knew she would be bruised. "Or are there any other *appointments* you wanted to make that we might have skipped over?"

Her head went up at that. He wasn't the only one with a temper, and Kate did not care for his tone of voice. Not at all.

"You're hurting me," she said deliberately, and with just a touch of disdain.

He released her immediately and bowed in imitation of an Italian gentleman. "Forgive me. I had no idea." He made a gesture toward the door. "Now, if you are ready . . ."

Kate was certainly *not* ready, not if he was going

to behave like this. She looked right into the green-gold eyes so full of gunpowder. "You needn't trouble yourself. I can find my own way home." But before she could turn away, his hand gripped her elbow again, more tightly than before.

"Like hell you will."

# Nine

Kate turned to face him very, very slowly. "You wouldn't care to repeat that?"

Mac was battling himself. Though their voices were low, he was aware they could easily draw the attention of this crowd. Finally, he made himself loosen his grip on her arm. "I never thought of you as a coward, Kate."

"A coward?" she repeated through clenched teeth. The man buried himself with every word.

"We are going to have one royal fight, Kate Polanski. You can run if you want, or you can come with me now."

He looked all of eight feet tall, and Kate suddenly remembered that her mother had always said you never knew a man until you saw him in a rage.

She straightened her shoulders, smiled a smile that was not friendly, and said, "I'll come." It was worth it to see Mac's face.

They had driven to Bel Air in Mac's aging BMW, and since it was quite obvious he adored the machine, Kate was doubly impressed when he ground the gears backing out of the Warwick drive. She sent him a rude glance to prove she'd noticed, then pulled her wrap closer around her and stared out the window.

Mac drove over the canyon to Kate's house, taking the twists and turns with just enough speed to make Kate hang on to the door as she tried to stay upright in the seat. She was in a slow burn by the time he pulled into her drive, and she had slammed the car door behind her before Mac had time to turn off the motor. He followed the trail of open doors to her living room.

"Well?" she said. She was standing in the center of the room, hands on hips, blue eyes filled with challenge.

"Why did you lie to me, Kate?"

She stiffened. Her hands tensed, then fell limply to her sides. It wasn't what she'd expected, and she couldn't have looked more guilty. She bit her lip and turned away, folding her arms protectively. "What do you mean?" she asked.

"You and Ferranti." He waited until she looked back at him. "You have some . . . connection to the man. What?"

Kate was trying to think of a way to begin.

"Are you lovers?" he asked, his voice strained.

"No!" she answered quickly, startled.

"Were you once?" His voice was more gentle now.

She shook her head. She had thought she'd have more time, that things would be more settled before they had this conversation. "Sit down with me. I can't tell you some of the story without telling all of it. It's . . . complicated."

He nodded cautiously.

She watched as he pulled his bow tie loose, unbuttoned two buttons, and sat on the edge of the couch. He controlled his expression beautifully, but Kate knew how much simmered just beneath that calm surface.

Her arms were still crossed. She felt as if they were all that was holding her in one piece.

"Come sit, Katie." He looked at her in a way that melted the ice in her spine.

Her own expression may have been pleading, or vulnerable. She didn't care. She only knew that she had hurt him, and it was the last thing she had wanted. She came to him, her steps uneven, and stood there silently until he dragged her down into his arms.

He hadn't intended to touch her, hadn't meant to kiss her with all these conflicting emotions boiling inside him. But when she had stood before him, head bent, her lovely face so uncertain, his arms had reached out of their own accord.

Her hands caressed his warm back beneath his jacket as he kissed her cheeks, her eyes, the pulse that beat in her fragile throat. Then his mouth found hers in a kiss that was both fierce and tender. When he drew back her lips felt swollen.

He cradled her head in one hand and teased a long strand of golden silk from its pins. The other arm was the anchor that held her against him. For the space of a few precious minutes they sat like that, and then he spoke.

"The truth, Kate."

She caught a breath, let it out in a slow sigh, and pulled away. But she grabbed his hands and held them tightly. "There's so much. I don't know . . . I suppose I should begin with World War II, or rather the end of the war in Italy." She ignored Mac's incomprehension and went on.

"Riccardo Ferranti was just a boy, fifteen when it was over. There had been war almost as long as he could remember, the poverty and hunger as much the enemy as any army. Survival was the only prize, and he had learned to be cunning, stealing food.

"Life was just as hard for so many Italians even after the liberation. People were living in bombed-out buildings, jobs were slow in coming, and still there was poverty and hunger. The jobs that were available went first to older men with families to support. Riccardo had no family left, but he lived with another boy and the boy's nine-year-old sister in the basement of what had once been a church. The boys were too old for an orphanage, too angry for charity. Together, they learned what and how to steal, what was of value. They studied and trained. In the next ten years they became quite famous. Art was their specialty.

"During those years, Riccardo's friend married and started a family. His sister, who was nineteen, and Riccardo had fallen in love and become engaged. But Riccardo didn't want to be a criminal when they married. They had saved enough to buy some land in the north, but there always had to be 'one more job.'" Kate shrugged. It was a hackneyed phrase.

"One night the police caught Riccardo leaving a house. He and his partner hadn't even gotten the painting they had come for. It had been moved. That was the last night either his partner or his fiancée ever saw him."

"What happened to him?" Mac asked.

She met his eyes. "I don't know."

"What do you mean? How did you find out this much?" Mac knew there was more she wasn't saying.

"Let me tell you what else I do know." She squeezed his hands. He nodded impatiently.

"They waited for weeks, and when there was nothing in the papers about his capture, the girl went to the police and reported him missing, hoping they could tell her something. But no one knew anything about him." Kate looked down then; it seemed she could almost feel the girl's bewilderment. "Mac, the girl's name was Gianetta, and she was pregnant with Riccardo's child."

His eyes changed. "What are you telling me?"

"I'm telling you that Riccardo Ferranti is my father. And tonight we met for the first time."

He looked as if he didn't believe her. "But your name is Polanski." This was crazy.

"My mother met an American woman named Polanski on the ship coming over. Mama thought it was a typical American name and changed hers so that no one would know she wasn't married."

"And your uncle Tony . . . a locksmith." Mac laughed wonderingly. Then he sobered and stared at her. "Why couldn't you have told me, Kate? I knew you were hiding something. Why couldn't you have trusted me?"

She stood up. She had to. Her stomach was knotted, her throat tight. "What would you have done if you'd known, Mac?" She whirled around before he had a chance to answer. "I'll tell you. You'd have told me I was using the paper for personal business. That I couldn't be impartial. And you would have been right.

"I pitched this story to Joe because it involved my father, and I wasn't secure enough simply to walk up to the man and introduce myself. I had to be sure I wanted to know him. I couldn't guess that Joe would take it seriously enough to put another reporter on it, or that there was already a theft involved." There was another reason she hadn't told Mac before, but she wasn't ready to say those words aloud to anyone.

"So you lied to me," he said. "Did you think I wouldn't care that you lied to me, Kate? When we lay in bed together did you wonder what I'd say when I found out? Did you think I wouldn't mind that you were using me as well as the paper?" He stood, dragging his hand through his hair. "Do you know what I was thinking tonight? I was thinking how crazy I was to let you go after every lead without me. I was mad at myself for not going for this story more strongly, not making my own leads, for being a sidelines reporter. But if you'd told me why, Kate, at least it would have been my choice." If she lived to be a hundred, she would remember the way he stared at her then. "You took away my choice and then slept in my arms, and that makes me damned angry."

He didn't look angry. He looked cold, cold and unfamiliar. Kate's eyes filled with tears, but no words came. What could she say? He was right. She'd never felt more wretched in her life.

"I'm sorry." Her voice sounded small.

"So am I." His answer seemed to come from far away. He turned his back to her and put both fists in his pockets. "I need time to think, Kate. Time alone."

It was a moment before she could speak. "All right." She waited, hoping there was something else, that he would say it would all work out some-how, that he just needed to be by himself for a while, that he'd call her in the morning.

But he said none of those things, and, as Kate heard the engine of the BMW, she felt as though something precious had been snatched right from her hands.


Mac found himself driving toward the beach. He needed the steady call of the ocean, the feel of cold salt air in his lungs. If he hadn't pressed, how long would it have been? he wondered. How many nights more would they have had together before she felt obliged to tell him?

He'd known, he'd always known, there was something.

And if their positions had been reversed, what would he have done?

It wasn't enough—the crash of the surf, the black sky and wet wind. Mac snatched a length of driftwood near his feet and hurled it into the waves with a kind of fury. He'd never in his life felt anger, real anger, toward a woman. He had been a master of indifference and had never even sensed that, until this moment. The women in his life had catered to his needs, spoiling him, demanding very little. Mac realized he had withheld himself from those women, never feeling they could share with him. Perhaps that was why he had never felt with other women the passion he felt with Kate.

She was fiercely independent. She could challenge a statement of his with a single glance, force him to look from another perspective with the lift of a brow. When she asked a question about a story he'd written, she found holes he hadn't seen before. Kate was not a passive partner. She matched his passion with her own, intellectually and physically. And she was beautiful. He found himself just staring at times, at the curve of her cheek or brow, the changing blue of her eyes, her pale skin, her soft rose mouth.

He remembered his mother as a gentle woman, who made intricate games out of mundane chores. She was very fair and very slender, always smiling or laughing. Mac was only eight when she died. His brother was already in college. Mac had missed her terribly.

Consuelo had come to them then, as housekeeper, nanny, and occasional general. She had fought with his father for things she thought Mac needed; Little League, Boy Scout camp, a stereo. Mac smiled at the memory of the tiny woman with the big voice, shaking her finger up at his father, announcing that it was time Simon noticed that he still had a son who needed him, that it was time to get on with life.

Simon MacHugh had stared hard at Consuelo, then turned and left the house without a word. But after that day his father found a thousand things for them to do together—fishing, ball games, Mac's science projects, drives to the country. When he couldn't get enough time off, Simon would put Mac in the Rambler and take him to story locations. Mac had loved those times best, his father rushing off to grab a story, talking to Mac on the way about what they might find, teaching him how to tell the story.

Mac wondered what his dad would do in his place. Then he turned, grinding his heel in the sand, and stalked to the car for his running gear.

The ride back over the hill was a rough one. Kate had just enough self-control not to think and to get into the car. She couldn't stop the tears that blurred her vision.

Once she had made it to the south side of the canyon, she pulled into the parking lot of a large chain coffee shop and turned on the inside car light to review the damage. Five minutes later she was back on the street, grateful she had thought to make the check. She had a sudden vision of a soggy blonde in bright pink crossing the Beverly Wilshire's lobby with black tattoos tracking her cheeks. She tried to smile at herself, but her face was too stiff.

The parking valet didn't blink an eye when she stepped out of the little white Volkswagen in full rig. He did look at her ankles, and gave a quick bow.

Somehow that exchange returned a sense of

normalcy to Kate. By the time she walked through the dark archway of the bar, she could think only of the meeting ahead.

*Her father.*

There he was, at a corner table along the banquette. As she drew nearer, Kate knew that he shared her expectation. His neck was stiffly angled, his hands holding tightly to both salt and pepper shakers. And when his face lifted to hers she saw it was true. He was as nervous as she.

Kate felt her lips curve. He was really here. She was a part of this man, and the sense of nature's tapestry was strong in her. There was another feeling as she looked down into the handsome, intelligent face, rich with character and subtlety. She knew the legacy of her mother's love for this man. It touched her in a way that was deep and unfathomable.

Kate realized, quite suddenly, that if he were guilty of wrongdoing, she would never write the story. Some degrees of professionalism were too much to ask.

He stood, and did nothing more than gaze at her. Then he smiled.

"Hello." His voice was low and warming.

A sweet, unreasoning joy flowed through her at the sound of his voice. It was no effort at all to smile back.

"Hello." There was a purity in her own voice. They were glad to see each other.

His smile turned self-conscious and he gestured to the other side of the corner table. "Will you sit?"

Kate wanted to laugh at the drawing room gesture, laugh that she was here at all, that the man before her was no imagined figure, but someone who could answer questions she'd had since she was old enough to form them. She sat down instead.

She looked at the table, the hastily abandoned salt and pepper shakers, the brandy snifter that held only one more sip.

"Am I late?" she asked anxiously.

His smile was rueful, and one finger touched the ballooned glass. "I am afraid I was early. I did not wish to take the chance that I might miss you."

Kate was mesmerized by the sight of those long fingers. Her startled gaze went from his hand to her own.

"Yes," he said. It was almost a whisper. "You have my hands."

She blinked quickly, but when he spoke again it was to the waiter. "Two cognacs." Silence filled the small space between them.

"I don't know what to call you," Kate blurted out at last.

His eyebrows rose slightly. "I, also, have wondered about that." He had a very distinctive voice, dark and commanding, but the slight accent softened each word. He moved the glass around on the white tablecloth. "Father?"

"Father," she said softly, and shook her head. "This is much harder than I thought it would be."

He touched her hand and took her breath away. "I am very happy you are here."

She turned her hand over. "Please don't say anything else just now. I'm afraid I'll cry." His hand was warm, firm, and supportive. Kate felt a strange echo of déjà vu.

The cognacs' arrival gave her a moment's reprieve, and she smiled shakily after her first sip. She was glad he didn't make a toast. A sensitive man.

She tried to imagine him as a young man, the

aggression more prominent, his intensity chan-
neled, emotions more visible. Masculine, strong.
And her mother, young enough to be shy, that
warm magic of her smile, love shining from her
eyes. The picture came with remarkable ease. They
would have been good together.

"You loved her," Kate said.

One eyebrow rose. "Do not doubt it." He gave
the words a wealth of meaning. Then he looked
toward the entrance of the bar as if he might see
Gianetta there. "She was everything to me. Everything of family. Everything of love."

"Please . . ." Kate took no notice of the strange
little catch in her voice. "What happened?"

Riccardo downed a great swallow from the glass
he held too tightly, then stared into the amber
liquid. "It comes to me in my dreams, that time."
He sighed heavily. "Life was nothing but sharp
edges then, edges of pain and pleasure. And more
vivid than death or hunger or safety was Gianetta.
When she laughed you had to laugh in answer.
Even as a child, she drew me." He smiled in memory. "She had a way of taking my hand in hers, as
if she were reassuring me, when I knew very well
how frightened she was. She cried in her sleep for
more than year after the war. But never in the
day, when someone might see.

"We lived in one room, Tonio and Gia and I, in a
basement that was crumbling around us. I would
listen to her cry in the night, and I dreamed of the
things I would buy her one day. She was so happy
with any toy we made her. I can still see her
playing in the ruins of the city, a child who had
seen too much. And then overnight she became
the woman of the house. Cooking for us, mend-
ing the rags we wore. Tonio and I were thieves.
'Hand and Glove' the police named us. We became
very good, and there was money for whatever we

needed. We found a little house outside of Roma, There Gia was queen.

"She was golden, like you, and very lovely. But too quiet. I would tease her, sometimes, just to watch her temper. Then one day, when she was seventeen, I came back from a job with a broken arm.

"She cried. For the first time in eight years, Gia cried like a baby, and she beat at me with her fists until I took her in my good arm and kissed her tears away." He laughed tenderly. "From that moment on I was hers." Riccardo looked into his daughter's eyes. "And she was mine.

"The next two years were the happiest in my life. Tonio knew, there were no secrets, and he, too, was in love. Then he got married, and took Gia to live with his wife. It was harder for us to be together after that."

He looked down. "Gia wanted to get married, but I kept telling her to wait until we had enough money to buy property for our vineyard. I did not want her to be tied to a thief."

Kate watched his expression turn bitter as he lifted his head. When he spoke again his voice was sad.

"I was a fool."

"What was it?" She had to ask, she had to know. "What happened to you?" Her hands gripped the edge of the table through the thick white tablecloth until they hurt.

"Why didn't she wait for me?" he asked instead.

"How could she? She was pregnant. You had disappeared. Months passed, they thought you had to be dead. The police would tell them nothing. Then Maria died in childbirth and Uncle Tony was crazy with grief. He and Mama decided that they had to leave the memories and make a new life. Mama told me stories of what it was like for an unmarried girl with a baby then. She saw how children were taunted on the streets.

"*Bastardo*. It's an ugly word in any language. . . ."

"So, they packed up the babies, Pietro and Angelo, and came to America to start again. Mama took the name Polanski and said she was a widow. She never married."

He couldn't believe it. "But she was so beautiful."

"She still is."

"*Che cosa—?*"

"You would have to ask her," Kate said slowly and deliberately. "You still haven't told me what happened the night you were caught."

"I was never taken by the police."

The words rocked her, and Kate felt a sound in her ears like the roaring of the sea. When her voice came, it was only a whisper. "But Uncle Tony . . . he said you were surrounded, that there was no way you could have escaped."

"He was wrong."

"Then *what happened*?"

"I climbed up to the roof from the outside of the house, and jumped to another roof, and another, until I was far enough away to go down to the street." He pushed his glass away and stared at a spot on the cloth beneath the ashtray. "I was on my way home when I realized I was tired of being hunted. I had lost my sense of self somewhere in all the running, in the game. So I contacted a policeman I knew had a special interest in me, and I turned myself in."

"But people cared for you, worried about you!" Kate couldn't believe he would hurt her mother that way.

"I assumed the authorities would let me make the call. But there was no privacy, and I was afraid they would trace Gia to Tonio, perhaps even think she was an accomplice."

"Mama said she reported you missing to the police. They didn't know anything about you."

Riccardo lifted a shoulder and shook his head. "The Italian police were not terribly organized at that time. I was in a cell in Roma for about ten hours before I was sent to France on an 'exchange program.' The French were very worldly about the matter. We made a deal involving certain unrecovered goods, and I was released after three years. But before then, I wrote to Tonio, several times. He never answered."

The silence was foggy. Kate was confused, her world changed by the things she had heard. If she was honest, she would have to admit that until a few minutes ago, she had believed that she, and her mother, had been abandoned by this man— despite the affection her family had for him.

"What happened when you got out . . . ?" She couldn't make herself say the rest. She hoped he wouldn't notice.

"I went home, and found no one." He looked away and said the words again. "No one. After that, I was drunk for days. When I came to, I visited my tailor and my shoemaker, who were quite happy to extend me credit. Then I called on a few of the homes and museums I had so successfully despoiled and told them I was the only man to protect them." He smiled slightly. "Eventually, I was hired by a millionaire with an appreciation of the ridiculous, and a very extensive private collection. That was the start of my life in business." Riccardo signaled the waiter and ordered a coffee, then looked at Kate, who shook her head. "I hired private detectives, but it was too late. There were no traces left."

After more than three years, that was not surprising.

Riccardo looked at Kate's hands, still holding

the edge of the table. "Now, Katerina, I want to know about Tonio, his children . . . and then I want to know about my daughter. What life has been like for her. Her dreams."

They talked for what seemed hours, and when the bar closed, they went to an all-night coffee shop. Kate told her father about the family, their successes and disappointments. She spoke of their fierce pride in each other, the bluff and blusterings of her uncle, and how Gianetta was still queen. They were a family, in an old-fashioned sense. That pleased Riccardo very much.

"I am glad the boys are happy and settled," he said.

Kate thought she knew where that was leading, but her father only waited. After a few seconds she grinned. "Excellent technique, Father. You pushed me right into that. Fortunately, I have used that tactic before myself."

"You like being a reporter." The corners of his mouth twitched upward beneath the sculpted mustache.

"It's great love and minor hate, but always interesting," she said, then laughed. "Fun."

Riccardo nodded. She might be the image of her mother, he thought, but there was something of him in her too. "And what of this partner of yours, the one who watches you so closely?"

Kate blushed deeply. How could she tell her father that Mac was her lover? "We fought tonight. He thinks I made a fool of him."

"Why would he think that?" Her father's eyes were kind. And because of that kindness, Kate found she wanted to tell him. When she had, he didn't judge or criticize. He only asked her, "What will you do now?"

Kate's voice revealed her doubt. "Hope he'll forgive me?" She could see the sun coming up, and there were so many things she still needed to know.

"Father, there are other things I have to ask."

"Sì, *bella*."

"I know about the theft of the Miao necklace. I know that the museum wants it kept out of the papers. It's the story I'm working on with Adam MacHugh."

Riccardo was suddenly alert, his back straight against the red vinyl booth. "Katerina, have you an ear for dialogue?"

She nodded.

"I want you to tell me exactly what Guy Jarré said to you. As much as you remember, word for word."

There was a long pause.

"How do you know I've spoken to Detective Jarré?" Kate finally asked, keeping her gaze on the design of the formica table.

"I know," was his only answer.

She looked across the table at him. She had spent the last few years of her life reading faces, situations, letting her instincts guide her actions. But those instincts were clouded now by emotion.

Right or wrong, he was her father. If, without conscience, without care, he used her, it was a lesson she would rather learn at cost. She would not withhold her trust from him. But she owed something to Guy Jarré.

"I don't think I can give you that information," she said at last. Her eyes apologized.

"You think I took the necklace?" He was very still, his expression amused.

"No."

He studied her carefully. "Then perhaps we can make a trade."

Kate smiled. Riccardo Ferranti had played chess-board ethics before. "Perhaps."

His answering smile was very pleased, and very charming. "It seems there is a condition, signorina?"

"Nonattribution. You are confined, in the same way I am, not to attribute the information to the source—or to relay what I tell you to anyone else."

"Done."

"And for my side?"

"*I* will answer your questions about the theft." He held out his hand.

Kate took it. "Done."

# Ten

"Detective Guy Jarré is a thief," Riccardo said quietly, after Kate relayed what she could remember of their conversation. "I see that I have shocked you. We were friends once, Jarré and I. But that friendship faded the first time he was tempted by the objects we had been hired to protect." Riccardo's smile was sad. "I was a thief for much of my life, Katerina. That life can be a drug—the danger, the greed, the power. Once you smell greed, you can never forget the scent of it, or the way it alters a man.

"Guy held a golden chalice in his hands one day, and his life was changed. He hates me because I know his weakness."

Kate was confused. "Did he try to take the chalice?"

"You don't understand, cara. He wanted that piece of gold so much that he could not even try to hide the desire from me. And in my business he had access to much, much more than one golden chalice. I could no longer trust him."

"What did you do?"

"I sent him out to do field work and kept my plans in the safe. It did not last long after that. He must have known I suspected him."

"Then he married?"

"Yes."

Kate couldn't understand. "But, Father, what if you were wrong? What if it was just a feeling— one that would go away in time?"

"This is not something for explanation, Kate." He reached for her hand. "It will not become more clear. I knew . . . and Guy saw that I knew." His logic was cruelly black and white, not compatible with the American legal system, but she never doubted his judgment.

She nodded slowly. "The Miao necklace?"

"That was made to look like the work of an amateur. I do not think so."

"Why do you think he told me about the theft?"

Riccardo shrugged. "I would guess he wants to keep me busy. For Guy, it was not enough to win at my game. He wants to discredit me."

Kate was intrigued by her father's lack of concern. "Do you think he'll try again at the exhibit?"

Riccardo grinned engagingly. "I plan to make it irresistible."

Kate laughed and pointed a finger at him. "*You* tell me everything."

Kate drove back over the canyon very cautiously. It was a sweet exhaustion that burned through her muscles, under her skin. She felt charged with adrenaline and caffeine and a strange, stinging happiness.

She did not think of Mac, or her father. It was her mother who occupied her thoughts. She wondered how Gina would feel when she found out what Kate had done, how she would look when she met Riccardo again for the first time in so many years. Would she be angry? The idea was crazy, but would they want, could there be, something between them after all these years?

Kate realized she hadn't asked her father if he had ever married. Suppose he had other children? She groped across the car seat for her purse. His phone number was inside. She was comforted, somehow, knowing that.

Only then did she let herself think of her father's plan. It would begin in a week. That meant she had a week to work things out with Mac. No matter what he thought or what he decided, she would make him understand, and if he could not understand, at least forgive. She had never before met a man who could touch her in the ways Mac did, her imagination, her logic, her senses. She had fallen in love with him, and she finally admitted it to herself.

Strange, she thought, that the two men who were the most important to her, father and lover, should come into her life now. Their appearances both sudden and dramatic, related and unrelated. Kate felt that any step she made was exceedingly important. Irrevocable. She wanted time to decide how to approach Mac, *and* her mother, *and* her uncle.

But now she had to get home and get out of this dress. Its silk felt like papier-mâché after so many hours.

She smiled to herself as she opened the front gate, thinking that the neighbors had been given quite a show lately, with Mac playing cat burglar and herself arriving home at seven in the morning in a very pink evening gown. She waved brightly at the house just across the way with the parted upstairs curtain.

"Morning, Mr. Garfield," she called. The curtain dropped in answer and Kate closed the gate behind her, plotting a series of *interesting* vignettes for Mr. Garfield's entertainment. Her book included politicians, cops, actors, musicians, waiters, strippers, gay and women's rights activists. Maybe she'd give a little tea, or a dress-like-a-cop party. Hmm, she did know some special-effects movie people, but they tended to get carried away with the explosives.

Between manufacturing ideas for the Garfield project and an icicle-cold shower, Kate managed to wake herself up enough to get through a morning at work. The afternoon might take some doing.

She downed two multivitamins with her coffee and ate a peanut butter sandwich, threw on some jeans, boots, a rag-tied muslin sweater, and was out the door in twenty more minutes. Makeup was saved for stoplights.

Mac spent the night in the beach house. After driving back to his place in town for a quick change and a shave, he had decided his next move. He called in to the paper, then headed to the L.A. County Museum and a very attractive redhead named Leslie.

"I cannot believe my eyes," Leslie said, laughing, when she saw Mac walking toward her desk. "Adam MacHugh, you have some nerve showing up here. The last time I saw you, you left me with a bottle of wine, a chateaubriand, and a seriously disturbed headwaiter." Leslie was tall and thin, with milk-white skin and a soft Virginia drawl she pulled out whenever she remembered.

"You look great, Les," Mac said, trying to distract her.

"You said you had to get a story on some guy who drove a Jeep through a bank window, then tried to rob it—because he was already there."

She was definitely holding a grudge, Mac thought, and grinned down at her. "I never lie. And it was page one. So, I owe you a good meal. Why don't you let me take you to Michael's for lunch?"

"I'm seeing someone," she said haughtily, but the smile spoiled it.

"Strictly business."

"Reporters," she said with great disgust, then crossed her legs and rocked her chair coyly. "Is there anything you wouldn't do for a story?"

"Oh, come on, Les." Mac pushed back his jacket to prop his hands on his hips. "You look like you're dying for caviar. You can let me spoil you, then you can help me with some information."

"I don't know." She tugged at a long strand of red hair. "It's a little early for lunch."

"Never too early for caviar. Of course, it might be too early for champagne, and lemon chicken is probably too heavy for a simple lunch."

"Mac," Leslie said conversationally, "you're standing in my way." He stepped backward gallantly. As she walked to the door she murmured indifferently, "You were just bluffing, you know I could never eat all that—Now, Adam MacHugh, you stop laughing or I'll pour my champagne all over that ratty notebook of yours."

It took a three-course lunch and a bit of coaxing, but he finally got Leslie to consent to give him the guest list he wanted. He had known, though, that after her first bite of chicken, she would have told him anything. So he waited for dessert before he sprang the big one.

"Leslie," he asked sweetly, "can you get me a look at the sign-in book for the last three weeks?"

Leslie suspended the bite she was about to take. "Look, Mac, the police were all over this stuff after that party. You're not going to find anything they didn't find. How'd you learn about it, anyway?"

Mac was suddenly serious. He and Leslie were

old friends, however little they saw of each other. "I need the favor, Les. If it's too much, tell me."

"All right, Mac." She grinned. "I know when to keep out of the way of reporter on a story. But let's keep this between you and me, okay?" She sighed, dabbed at her mouth with the yellow napkin, and placed it beside her plate. "Nice lunch."

"Come on, will you?" Mac was all teasing impatience. He wanted to see the scene of the crime.

"It's quiet today," Leslie said as she led Mac to the storage floor. There were no guards, no visitors, just the sound of Leslie's keys and the click of her heels against the hard floor. "If we see someone, go along with whatever I say." Mac nodded.

The storage area looked like any other warehouse basement, but the doors were double, widely spaced, and numbered, with small computer key units outside each door.

"How difficult would it be to duplicate one of these key cards, Les?"

"If someone knew our system and had the code, easy. The way they got into the China exhibit was a little different. It was just up here." She led him one door farther. The computer link beside the door was burn-blackened.

"What about the alarm system?" Mac asked, examining all around the door. There were scratches where the doors had been pried open.

"Oh, it went off all right—with a delayed-action timer."

"Interesting."

Leslie pulled at a bit of blackened wire. "Whoever did it knew enough to short the alarm system. But why the timer?"

Mac brushed his hands together and pulled Leslie back down the hall. "Got to see that sign-in book. Better yet, photocopy it!"


It was one o'clock by the time Mac made it to the paper. Kate looked up from her computer terminal to see him talking to Joe outside his office. Joe nodded and bellowed "Kate!" in her direction. Then both men went into the glass-walled office.

Kate shut off the computer, grabbed her notes, and hurried over. Inside, Mac was sitting with a legal-size photocopy of what looked like a long list of names. Joe was leaning back in his wide chair, one hand fumbling for his cigarettes.

Mac lifted his gaze to Kate, but she could read nothing.

"Mac thinks he found something at the museum, Kate," Joe said as he lit a match.

Mac laid the sheet of paper across the desk so that both Kate and Joe could read it. "We may have a suspect," Mac said. "Kate, remember what you said about having the feeling that Jarré gave off a lot of undercurrents about Ferranti?"

Kate nodded.

"Well," Mac went on, "I found out that Jarré wasn't invited to that party at the museum until the day before, and he arranged the invitation himself. The exhibit arrived on Thursday, the party was Saturday. Ferranti was in and out of the museum six or seven times." He pointed to the signatures. "Jarré arrived for the first time on Friday. He told the guard he was meeting Ferranti, but Ferranti didn't come to the museum until two hours later, after Jarré had already left. Saturday, Jarré came to the party with his wife. But she had to leave early. And whoever stole the necklace rigged the museum alarm to go off with a timer set to the time they chose. That time was forty minutes after Mrs. Jarré went home. It's suspicious."

"Ferranti is certain it was Jarré," Kate said quietly.

"You spoke to him?" Joe asked abruptly.

"I met him late last night." Kate took a deep breath, sensing Mac's interest. "Joe, before I go any further, there's something else I had better explain, or rather, confess." She looked across the desk into those sharp gray eyes. "You're not going to like it."

Kate dove right in, describing the complications of her relationship with Riccardo Ferranti, and then her father's suspicion of Guy Jarré. But before she could relate the trap Riccardo had planned, Joe interrupted.

"You're off the story."

There was an awful silence.

Kate was the first to speak. "You have every right to be angry, Joe. I understand that I—"

"Do you understand the policy of this paper, Kate?" Joe sat forward to lean on his desk, his expression grim. "Your personal involvement in this story makes you ineligible. Apart from the insult to me as an editor—and as a friend—I think your behavior in this matter has been unethical in the extreme. How can a newspaper maintain a standard of objectivity if its reporters are writing stories about their damned relatives?" Here Joe allowed himself a small show of temper, then he tightened his control. "Give your notes to Mac, then see Tom for something else."

Kate was on her feet in an instant."No, Joe. I'm sorry, really, but it's gone this far—"

"And it never should have. That's all, Kate. No more argument."

She stood there a moment longer, as if she couldn't quite believe what had happened. Then she turned and walked out to the newsroom. But as she neared her desk she knew she couldn't face sitting there, thinking about the mess she had made of everything. She veered to the assistant editor's desk.

"Tom," she said before she was within two feet of his desk, "Joe said to see you for an assignment. Have you got anything I can go right out with."

Tom shuffled a few papers and pulled one. "Sure, Kate. Take a photog to this press conference in Hollywood. They've set up two candidates for city council in a debate—and they're married to each other."

"You're not looking for something really cute, are you?" Kate asked tiredly.

Tom shrugged. "Yeah, maybe something along the lines of *Adam's Rib* Battle-of-the-sexes stuff."

"Great." Kate gave up and snatched the address from his hand. She was on her way to the elevators when Mac came out of Joe's office. He looked right into her eyes. Kate slowed, then quickened her pace to the elevators. She still had to find a photographer who was free.

Kate wrote Tom the cute piece he wanted, sandwiching in the issues discussed in the debate. Then, twenty minutes before deadline, she rewrote the story to her own taste.

"Tom," she called over to his desk, "I'm ready. But do me a favor and read the second version before you make a decision."

"They both on line?" he asked. She nodded, and he said, "You got it."

Kate was free to go home.

Mac had been away from the paper the rest of the day. For that, Kate had been grateful. But she couldn't help wondering where he was, and she still hadn't turned over any notes to him. She hadn't filed them on the computer.

At home, she made a cup of tea and drew a hot bath, filling the air with clouds of scent. Submerged to the neck, she let the heat soak through her, hoping it would wash some of the misery away. She wished she could call someone, but the people she wanted to talk to were all family. Even Marianna was too close.

She'd been wrong. Kate knew it. But she was tired of being told so, and feeling worse with every telling. It was a lesson learned. She sat up in the tub, reaching for the soap. Where was her backbone?

She'd made a mistake, not fatal, not unforgivable, just a stupid, emotional gamble. She wouldn't make that kind of mistake again, and whether or not Joe or Mac forgave her, she needed to forgive herself.

By the time she pulled herself out of the tub, she was walking with her eyes almost closed. She was too tired to eat, too tired to dry her hair. All she wanted was ten hours of sleep. But even in her half stupor, she went to the front door and unlocked it, just in case Mac decided to come and she couldn't hear the bell. Then she stumbled back to the bedroom, dropped her robe on the floor, and fell into bed.

Mac was at Riccardo Ferranti's canyon house for half an hour before the dark Mercedes turned into the drive that evening. Mac would have left for home at dusk if he hadn't fallen asleep, but he only woke with the sound of the finely tuned engine. He started his own engine and pulled up beside Ferranti's car in the garage.

A great shadow climbed out of the Mercedes to stand threateningly beside it, but Mac was already at the car's back window. "Mr. Ferranti," he said in a sure and low voice, "I'm Adam MacHugh from the *L.A. Daily*. We met at the Warwick party." His eyes began to adjust to the darkness of the garage. "I wonder if I might have a few words with you."

Riccardo regarded the man. He was lean in an athletic sense, handsome, his features strong and regular. He wore a light sport coat and open shirt. His large hands were barely curled at his sides. Opening the door, Riccardo stepped out of the car, smiling a half smile, and signaled to Andrew. "Come inside, Mr. MacHugh. I am very pleased to see you again."

Mac raised one brow, and followed the two men up the stairs.

The house was tastefully, expensively furnished, yet coolly impersonal in the way of a rental. Mac looked around, unconsciously searching for clues to the man. On a coffee table was a thick, colorful book on China and two magazines, *World News* and something in Italian. There seemed to be nothing else of a personal nature, and Mac knew instinctively that the paintings had come with the house. He filed the information away.

Riccardo led him to the center of the living room and gestured to a comfortable chair. "Would you care for a drink, Mr. MacHugh, or perhaps coffee?"

"I would love some coffee, thank you," Mac answered easily. He wondered how long he'd been sleeping, but didn't want to be caught looking at his watch.

"Andrew." Riccardo turned to the giant who stood nearby. "Could we have two coffees, please?"

The man nodded, his eyes flickering to Riccardo

and back again to Mac. Riccardo seemed amused. The large man moved toward the kitchen. "And, Andrew . . ." Riccardo waited for the other man to turn. "Please join us, if you like." The man hesitated, then continued to the kitchen.

"Andrew does not care for reporters as a rule," Riccardo said philosophically. "But in time . . ." Mac had a moment to wonder what was meant by that. Strangely, he felt that Riccardo was not referring to Kate.

"You followed me?" Riccardo asked, settling into a corner of the sofa.

"Another night," Mac said.

"Ah, I shall have to warn Andrew that we must take more care. He is usually quite expert in eluding surveillance."

Mac couldn't help but smile. "You haven't seen Kate drive." He was amazed how comfortable he felt with this man.

"My daughter is a most interesting woman."

Mac didn't answer, but his expression was suddenly serious.

"Kate said that you and she are partners, Mr. MacHugh," Riccardo said, giving him the opening.

"Call me Mac."

Riccardo smiled, transforming the pirate features. "Mac, and you must call me Riccardo."

"Riccardo, Kate has been taken off the story," Mac said, "and she is not terribly pleased. She should never have involved herself in a story about a relative. But Kate knows that."

Riccardo nodded once. "There are rules in every profession."

"Now," Mac went on, "I'm left with the pieces."

"You have questions." Riccardo looked up as Andrew entered the room with a silver tray containing cups of espresso, a bottle of Sambucca, and two glasses.

Mac watched with interest as Andrew poured the liqueur. In each glass were three coffee beans. "We call them 'little flies,'" Riccardo said. "They flavor the Sambucca." Andrew lit a match to the surface of the liquid. "If they remain whole, they bring great luck. You do not join us, Andrew?" Andrew only scowled in answer, then turned and left. Riccardo laughed. "Andrew is my old friend, who worries too much about my consequence." The flames flickered and died. Riccardo raised his glass. "To my daughter, Katerina Maria Ferranti."

Mac grinned, repeating, "Katerina Maria Ferranti," and drank.

"Now, Mac, you have questions?"

"About Guy Jarré." Mac pulled his pad and pen from his coat pocket.

Later, Mac might wonder at the amount of information he was given, but at this moment he was too grateful. When Riccardo spoke of his plans to trap Jarré, Mac interrupted.

"Did you tell Kate all this?" he asked.

"Certainly." Riccardo was undisturbed. "Why not?"

"Why not?" Mac shook his head. "Riccardo, your daughter is a reporter, and a stubborn daredevil. She wouldn't miss an opportunity to record this!"

Riccardo grinned. "Hmm, I understand what you mean. Perhaps we can see that she's kept busy."

Mac looked down and cleared his throat uneasily. "I can't lie to her, Riccardo. I'm already on Kate's black list. I was . . . uh, given a story of hers once before."

At eleven the next morning Kate was at her desk, nursing a cold cup of coffee and a colder story. She looked up over the rim of the cup and saw Mac striding down the aisle. He was coming right toward her. She jumped and his large hand reached out to steady her cup, then took it from her and placed it safely on the desk.

Her head went back as she met his eyes.

"We need to talk," he said in an even voice. Her stomach was tight as a drum, her heart fearful. Her own eyes were questioning. His blond head moved left in a small gesture, then back.

Kate stood, brushed nervously at her trousers, and followed him. She wondered where he was leading her, then rushed to stay even five feet behind him. When he went through the door to the stairs, she had to run the last few feet to see if he went up or down. Up?

She was breathing fast by the time she reached the door two stories above. Through the door's rectangular window she saw Mac talking to a secretary. Then he walked into Jack Kelsoe's office, leaving the heavy door open behind him.

Why would Mac be taking her to see the director of display advertising? she wondered.

Timid now, she pulled open the stairway door and walked past the secretary's desk, through to Jack's office. No one was there. She waited, wincing only at the soft sound of the door closing behind her. There was the click of a lock, the soft thud of footfalls on carpet.

When she opened her eyes she had to look way, way up at the man standing inches from her.

"Never again," he said in a warm, gravelly voice. His big hands closed over her arms. His gaze raked up, then down the length of her. "Say it."

"Never again," she whispered.

He studied her face for a tense moment, then said with flat impatience, "I swear, Kate, if you ever lie to me again, I'll—"

"Mac." She threw her arms around him. The

kiss was hard and sweet. Welcoming. Warming. "The longest time, years, it seems, without you," she murmured between kisses.

"Kate. Katie, my girl." His arms banded tightly around her until she was lifted from the floor. His lips burned hers, his tongue sweeping her mouth with warm, possessive strokes. He turned completely around and Kate never noticed. She was lost in a world of dark, unexpected emotion. Her skin was alive in anticipation of his touch, her blood rushing in all directions at once, her brain clouded with sweet, drugging desire.

She clung to his shoulders, then caressed them as he lowered her feet to the floor. Her palms brushed over the warm cotton of his shirt, down to his waist then around his hips. He gave a low groan, pressing against her soft stomach, and she pushed back instinctively. His hands stroked her shoulders and along her arms in a quick, exploring motion, almost as if he were reassuring himself she would feel the same.

"How I want you, Kate," he whispered urgently. His hands cupped the sides of her neck, thumbs along her jaw. "In my bed, in my life." He rubbed his face in her hair. "I want to fight with you, or for you, to be there." Her heart turned over at the words, so much more than she had expected. "Kate." He gave her a little shake. "We haven't had much time, but I want all of it. I want you to care enough about me to give me honesty." His thumbs traced the softness of her lips. "Can we have that, Kate? Can we try?"

"Yes," she said simply. "Please, yes."

# Eleven

"We can't do this," Mac said. His breath was hot and quick, his hands busy. He was aggression without offense, and he knew very well how, and where, to touch her with the greatest effect. Her jacquard silk blouse feathered against her skin with his caresses. The scent of him was warm, familiar. His mouth on hers threw flashes into every part of her body.

"Mac." Kate sighed as one of his hands moved on her breast. Hers were searching, stroking.

"If we . . . No . . . no. Not here." He gripped her arms, pushing her away from him with slow self-restraint. Their lips were the last contact, then she swayed toward him, and his hands returned to steady her.

"Katie, help me." He groaned and dragged her hand to the heat of his mouth. Her blue eyes were liquid as they stared into his.

"I want you," she whispered, "and I lose my mind when I'm with you. So don't ask me for help."

His eyes burned and laughed at the same time. In one quick turn he left her. His back to her, running both hands through his hair, he said, "I'm dying, Katie, dying. How do you do this to me?" Then he whipped around to face her. "Get off early."

She grinned. "I'll tell Joe you asked it as a bonus for that museum photocopy." Her hands were flexing, aching to touch him again.

"If that's what it takes," he said, one corner of his mouth rising. "You go first." He gestured toward the door.

"No, you go first," she teased, hands on hips.

"Very funny, Polanski," he growled. "But if you don't go, you won't be going."

Kate detoured to the ladies' room for repairs before returning to her desk. Mac was already working at his terminal. Rob was observing both of them with an ill-disguised eagle eye, and for the sake of the games, she pretended indifference; no more than glancing Rob's way.

Kate spent the next several hours holding the phone with her shoulder as she worked at her terminal. Finally it was six o'clock. Mac had disappeared some time ago and had yet to return. But Kate knew he'd find her. She treasured the anticipation, wondering at her happiness.

She turned over her desk to the night shift, locking the drawer that was hers, and walked beside Rob to the elevator.

"Why, Kate," he said, feigning surprise. "You're such a little thing, I hardly saw you there."

She grinned and shook her head. "Rot," she said, looking straight ahead. "You got a message for me, Robert?"

"Could be." He held the elevator door open as she eyed his homely-beautiful face with annoyance. "Could be that Mac said he'd meet you at your house at seven-thirty, even if you made him climb Rapunzel's wall again."

Kate knew very well Rob must've been told that story. "I'm gonna find you a girl, Rob," she said as he punched the lobby button. "Someone to mow you down to size."

"You know a woman who could handle this mug?"

She looked at the man with new perspective. Was it possible that Rob thought she hadn't gone out with him because of his face? she wondered. He had a strong, well-built body, and an attitude of mocking self-confidence that was very sexy. He was unafraid to have a man who looked like Mac as his closest friend. Did he think women looked no farther than a face?

"There's something wonderful about that mug, Robert," she said. She let her gaze caress his rough, weathered features, the well-marked lines fanning out from his blue-green eyes.

Rob read her approval, her genuine liking for him, then said, "You ever need a hand with him, you just let me know, Katie. I'll straighten the guy out."

She gave him an interested look. "Think you could?"

Rob grinned. "Uh-huh."

Kate tried not to laugh. "That's nice to know." There was no sexual spark between them. Rob had muffled it as soon as he'd seen the first indications that she and Mac were involved. That earned him Kate's respect. A glance around showed her that the two other people in the elevator she knew only by sight.

"Has he ever stuck to just one, Rob?" she asked quietly. He might tell her to mind her own business, or to ask Mac herself, but he might give her an answer. He didn't speak at first. The elevator stopped with a small jolt, and they walked together to the parking lot.

Rob looked down at the woman beside him, trying to decide what to say. Mac wouldn't like it.

He'd want to tell her himself. But if there was no answer now, she might form her own conclusions. Rob gave in. "He did stick to just one once," he said, "but it didn't work." Her blue eyes asked the question. He shrugged. "Just wasn't meant."

Kate looked away quickly, letting his words echo in her mind.

"How 'bout you, Katie?"

The question surprised her. She looked up at the sandy-haired man and wondered if he asked for Mac or for his own curiosity. "Once," she said shortly, but without rancor. "But the man couldn't stop looking for . . . whatever it was he was looking for." They were near her car now. Rob had walked past his own to continue the conversation. He took the keys from her hand, opened the door, returned the keys, and slammed the door shut after she was inside. Kate smiled at the small, unconscious courtesies, and rolled down the window.

"There are all kinds of fools, Kate," Rob said, smiling as he bent down.

"I'm gonna find you that girl, Rob," she said, and laughed softly. She was glad Mac had a friend like this one.

"For love or punishment?" he asked warily, straightening.

"Both." She started her little car, backed out, and waved as she drove off.


At home Kate took a quick shower, then stepped into a lounging robe of a soft cotton weave. It was a pure and fresh white, and seemed to melt the day's weariness.

She had a man, she thought, as she brushed her hair at the mirror. The strokes were long, rhythmic, pulling her head to the side. She had never thought of herself as particularly vain, but now she touched her own cheeks, searching her reflection. All her life she had dismissed the compliments. Because of her family, she had a strong sense of her own worth, the inside Kate. She had never understood what people saw when they looked at her. She didn't see herself as so unusual looking. But now she studied her image more carefully.

This woman, the one in the mirror, had a lover, a man who wanted her, wanted to be with her.

She told herself it wasn't nerves she felt, just tension. They still had a lot to talk about, much to work out. She wouldn't be able to stand it if her stories continued to land in his lap. She could try to pretend it didn't matter, but it would still abrade. And she knew it would take time and tests for Mac to believe in her. She didn't like it, but she was the one who had been in the wrong. Now she would have to prove herself.

And there was the future. She thought back over the words he had said to her. They were words of commitment. But what kind of commitment? She knew he was possessive of her. He'd shown it in all the small ways, from a look in his eyes, to the way he'd reach over her head to open a door, or the caress that wouldn't leave her when they had long since finished making love. What did he want?

Kate was certain that, for her, there was no going back. She was in love. It poured through her every time she saw his beautiful face. He was so much more than just the physical, though, that the sight of him always reminded her of the things he shared with no one else, things saved to share with her. There were times when she could almost feel that barrier go down like a tangible wall.

In the kitchen she pulled steaks from the freezer, salad makings from the fridge. It was time, she thought as she looked up at the kitchen clock. He should be here. Suddenly, she was impatient.

Where was he?

Only a few minutes later, holding a knife in her fist, she turned at the sound of the front gate closing. She waited, listening. The front door was pushed open. She turned full face.

"I'm not that late," he said, looking with amusement at the knife in her hand. She dropped it to the cutting board, and moved to the sink to rinse her hands. Her hair fell over one shoulder as she bent her head. Then she felt his warm, vital heat leaning into her. His kiss fell just behind her ear.

"My Kate, shy?" he whispered wonderingly. His hands were at her waist, running lightly back and forth above her hips, then dipping to skim down over them. She nodded once.

"Why, honey?" He crossed his arms at her waist to hold her closer. She shrugged. He rocked her silently for a moment, his chin resting on her head.

Kate drew from his warmth, his strength, grateful that he didn't demand an answer she didn't have. Never before had she needed another's support. Her family had always remarked on her independence. She had rarely gone to them with her problems. If difficulties occurred at school or with friends, she would work them out, then come home with the story of how she had handled things, for better or worse. She'd been a loner, content with her own company. Suddenly she was finding that she needed this man, needed *his* company, his words and thoughts around her. When he wasn't there, she almost felt there was something wrong or out of sync. As if it were some rare disease, she was reluctant to face what she thought of as her dependence.

"You feel so good in my arms," he whispered, hugging her. Did he know what it did to her when he said things like that? she wondered. Could he know how limitless it made her world seem?

"Mac," she said softly.

He bent closer, curling his body around hers. "Mmm?"

"I . . . Does it scare you, what we have—what we've begun?"

His hands held hers, one of his thumbs stroking her knuckles, back and forth. "More than you could imagine," he answered her, staring down at their hands. Then his beautiful mouth turned up at each corner. "But I comfort myself with the thought that *you've* got to be as scared as I am."

The breath she'd held so tightly suddenly escaped on a laugh. She closed her eyes and said quickly, "I'm glad you're home, Mac."

He turned her in his arms and bent his head to place a gentle kiss on her lips. "So am I, Katie. So am I."

She reached up and thought how sweet it was to hold him just so. Their breathing shallow, they both looked long into each other's eyes, trying to read all that could be seen there.

"You've never even taken me out to dinner," she said nonsensically as she tried to memorize each line of his face, the textures of his skin, the curve of his lips.

"Dinner?" His mouth brushed lightly over the corner of hers. "Okay." His lips feathered her cheek, then her jaw and down the curve of her neck. She felt his chest expand as he drew in her scent, then he pulled her hips against his with an urgency she found as exciting as the most intimate caress.

This time when his lips met hers, the kiss was

impatient, frankly sexual. He was not gentle, but she didn't want him to be. His tongue explored her mouth with silken heat. She shuddered in response. She couldn't get enough air into her lungs, and was dizzy from the lack of it. Her fingers tangled in his soft blond waves, then turned to fists when he slipped a hand through the wide arm of her caftan and found her bare breast. He gave a low groan as he filled his hand with her. Then, in a startling rush, he pulled away, only to lift her high in his arms and stalk toward the bedroom.

Beside the bed, he set her on her feet, his eyes searching hers for a reflection of his need. When he found it he smiled a wide smile of pure sensual pleasure. Then he tugged the caftan up and over her head in one move. His green-gold eyes stayed locked with hers as he lifted the garment and buried his nose and mouth in it. He breathed deeply, then let it slide to the floor. There was something so carnal in the gesture, so shocking, that Kate froze, her chest and neck flushing with excitement.

Mac bent to lick one breast, then the other. He touched his thumb to her mouth and backed up a step to shrug out of his jacket, unbutton his shirt.

Kate knew she was trembling, but she had no need to control it. This was her lover, her love, and she could show him that he made her weak.

Naked, richly contoured, and proud, he stood only two feet from her. Kate felt her arms reaching for him before she even had the thought. He stepped into them, letting his flesh glide warmly against hers.

"Mac." Her eyelids were heavy, her face hot. Her lips pressed against the skin of his shoulder, and her eyes closed. His mouth followed the curve of her neck to her breast and he knelt to suckle there. His hands cupped her buttocks, squeezing rhythmically, and she felt him tugging down the last bit of lace that covered her. While his mouth moved to the other breast, one hand parted her thighs to caress upward, his stroking sending blood rushing to her head and weakening her knees. Gently, he nudged her backward until she felt the edge of the bed. Again, his head gave a small push, and she sat. His mouth returned to hers as he knelt on the floor between her legs. It was a blind man's kiss, testing, exploring, as if he had never kissed her before. When he had made her frantic for more, he gentled the kiss and pushed her flat on the bed, parting her thighs farther. His eyes held hers with a look she didn't understand, and he lowered his head.

His mouth was liquid heat, and her hips arched upward in helpless response until he pulled her legs over his shoulders. Her restless fingers caught at the coverlet, twisting it, then they sought his shoulders, his hair.

His hands beneath her, he took her to the edge, only to withdraw. When she called to him, he gave her tiny flicks of his tongue, then kisses that played fire. Once more he made her wait. Then, when his mouth caressed her again, she knew nothing but her own pleasure, until he filled her.

He whispered to her, kissing her ear, her mouth, telling her how it felt to be inside her, how lovely he found her. All the while his hands skimmed over her, shifting position, rhythm. Hers waded through the hair on his chest, over his sensitive back and hips, his legs. She didn't believe she could contain the things he made her feel, but she wanted it to go on forever. The bed rocked, and they laughed gaspingly at the sound. Kate cried out once more, and Mac almost shouted at the end.

And they both knew that it was more than it had ever been, that they were loved.

"Were you ever in love before?" Mac asked, cuddling her head against his shoulder.

"I thought I was, once."

He didn't like the sound of her voice. "What happened?"

"Oh, it was wrong, just wrong. Tell me about you."

He sighed. "I thought I might have been in love once before." He paused. "We were better friends than lovers. We're still friends. I'd like you to meet her sometime."

Kate tried to think about how she might feel, meeting a woman Mac had made love to. The idea put her in a mild panic.

She pulled at the curls below his collarbone. "If I feed you, can we have a serious talk?" she asked.

"Depends on what you're offering."

"Steak?"

There was a moment of thoughtful silence. "Rare?"

"Any way you want it." Her laughter was muffled by his chest.

"Kate." He took a deep breath. "I think I'm in love with you."

The world went still. "Then we're very lucky," she said softly.

"Tell me." His hands ran urgently over her body.

"I love you," she said, self-consciously. She rubbed her cheek against his smooth shoulder and threw her head back, laughing. "I love you."

The steaks were on the grill outside. Mac was tending them, fork and spatula held in salute.

Kate looked out the window as she set the table. Mac was staring at the grill as if waiting for a buzzer to go off.

"Hey you!" She stuck her head out the kitchen door. Mac jerked toward her. "Turn 'em," she said, laughing.

"Right," he said, looking at the grill, getting ready for the tackle. But he made sure she wasn't watching when he did it.

Five minutes later they were sitting down to eat. Mac was terribly smug. Kate loved it.

"So," she said, cutting the meat quite carefully, "you want my notes, Mac?"

He stopped, a bite halfway to his mouth, and scowled at her.

"You don't have to do that."

She threw him an impatient look. "You want them or not?"

He thought it over for a minute. "Wouldn't hurt." His grin came slowly, then was gone. "I'm sorry you're off the story, Katie."

She shrugged one shoulder, but wouldn't look at him. "I suppose I deserved it."

"Yeah." His voice was low, but matter-of-fact. So was the kick she gave him.

"You're really going to give me your notes?" he asked, absently rubbing his shin.

One eyebrow rose. "Did you think I'd want to sabotage you?"

"No, of course not." He reached a hand for hers, and she softened immediately. "I went to see your father today. I liked him, Kate." Her head snapped back, and Mac spent a moment thinking how beautiful she looked, her eyes so deep a blue, her fair skin glowing "He told me about his plan for Jarré next week. You think it'll work?"

"I think it depends on too many things to know, but it should be interesting. Did he tell you how he wants to bait the trap?"

"He said Jarré found him the warehouse, and that he planned to file a security blueprint with the owner, a friend of Jarré's. Then he'll ask Jarré to set up surveillance from the Beverly Hills crime prevention unit after delivery." Mac played with his salad as if exploring a plate of rocks, before moving back to the safety of pure beef. "He thinks Jarré will delay the surveillance and make the attempt. Riccardo plans to be waiting, cameras rolling. That, and my photocopy of the sign-in book, should set him."

"That was good work, Mac," Kate said seriously, then continued as Mac pretended to gloat. "Did my father show you the camera model he wants to use?" She speared a water chestnut in her salad. Mac watched her bite it as if afraid for her. He shook his head no. "The whole apparatus is no bigger than my little finger and beautifully camouflaged. I'm going to weasel my way into the monitor truck."

Good, he thought. At least she'd be out of harm's way. "That what you wanted to talk about?"

She bit her lip, then took a sip of cranberry juice. She hoped he'd understand. "No. I don't like demands, Mac. I won't make them. But this is the second story of mine you've ended up with." She didn't really know what to say next.

"You want me to turn it over to someone else, Kate?" He had stopped eating, or moving at all.

"No, Mac. No," she said quickly. He relaxed. "I just . . ." She flushed, then shook her head. "No. Never mind."

His hand lifted her chin until her eyes met his. "I won't let it happen again, if that helps, love." She smiled gratefully, and his thumb stroked her jaw once before he went back to his dinner.

"Great steak," he said.

She grinned. "Great salad." His bare foot covered hers.

# *Twelve*

They had that week. The days were hard work, fresh news, and stray glances. The nights were perfect, long and full of love, the scent of jasmine always in the air. Kate had never felt so alive, had never thought she could love so much or so well. She was often distracted, and the sound of her laughter was sweet.

Mac didn't bother to analyze. For him it was simple. He finally had what he needed in his world, this woman. He wrote better than ever before, his senses and instincts keener. He was better, in fact, at everything.

On Thursday, Kate picked up her phone and dialed Mac, three desks away. He was arguing county politics with Rob.

"Yah. MacHugh here."

"I've been asked to bring you to Sunday dinner," Kate said.

Mac looked up to see her crossing her legs with a strategic placement of the slit in her black skirt. He paused a moment for appreciation, and said, "That one's my favorite. The right thigh." Kate gave a start he could see from his desk, then hastily rearranged her skirt. "The left is nice, of course," Mac went on, "but there's something about the right that's special."

"Careful, Mac, *I* know where you're ticklish."

"The woman is evil, truly."

She tried to get back to the point. "About Sunday."

"From whence does this 'invitation' come?"

"Well . . ." She decided to draw it out. "It started with my mother, then Uncle Tony came on the phone long enough to tell me that he liked you." She waited for that to sink in.

Mac leaned back in his own chair. "Now, I *am* flattered."

"Mac."

"No, I mean it. I'm flattered. How did you twist his arm?"

"You passed his test. He really is the classic 'all bark, no bite,' you know." Kate propped her chin in one hand and swung her chair around so that she was facing his desk. The slit widened as she recrossed her legs. "Besides, you're a Lakers fan." She spun back to face front and waited, but there was no response. "Mac?"

Kate jumped as a large hand reached out to her skirt and pulled it tidily closed. She looked up, phone still in hand.

"Why, hello," she said.

Mac grunted in answer.

"What?" she asked innocently, putting down the phone.

But just then, Joe came out of his office barking, "Mac, aren't you finished with that pipeline story yet?"

"Five minutes," Mac answered. Joe scowled at Mac, then Kate, then turned back to his glass office. "When you two gonna make up, anyway?" Mac asked Kate.

She sighed deeply. "Not until I apologize, I'm afraid." She pushed back her chair and stood. "Wish me luck." Mac watched her walk away, his expression tender.

"Subtle, MacHugh," Rob said with a laugh from just behind him. "This love affair is the worst-kept secret since McCarthy's blacklist."

Kate stood at Joe's open door and knocked. "Got a minute?" Joe nodded. Kate thought she had seen him look more approachable.

Half an hour later, Kate left Joe's office feeling that peace had been reestablished. Joe was a close friend. It was good to have him back.

Friday, Kate was busy with interviews all day, but Friday night Mac took her to dinner and the theater. There was a misting breeze late that night and they hurried home to cocoa and a fire.

Saturday, Kate helped Mac shop for new furniture for the beach house. "I think we'll be sharing it soon, anyway," he had mumbled in invitation. Kate didn't want to think, yet, of those major changes. She tried to keep the conversation on colors and shapes.

For two hours that day he pretended to be fascinated by the most horrible objets d'art, until Kate agreed enthusiastically about a futuristic steel chandelier. It had spikes. After that he pushed Kate toward the couches on display.

"When do you move in?" she asked him, as he bounced up and down on a lovely taupe Ultrasuede couch.

"Next week. You volunteering?"

"What's in it for me?"

He grabbed her wrist and tugged her down to bounce beside him. "Pizza and beer, and I'll teach you how to body surf."

"Okay. This the one you want, Mac?"

"One more test." He pulled her into his arms, amazing her with the number of arms and legs he had. Then he kissed her thoroughly. "This is the one," he said softly to her, then he looked at the salesman looming above them. "We'll take it."

And then it was Sunday.

The sky was clear blue, but the sun wasn't nearly bright enough to warrant Mac's very dark glasses.

"You nervous?" she asked him as they walked from her house to the car.

"Oh, no," he said casually. "Let's take your car. My hands won't unclench long enough for me to hold the wheel."

"Idiot." She laughed and pushed the glasses down on his nose.

The living room curtain of the big house was pushed aside as they rolled up the drive. "That's Uncle Tony," Kate explained. "Marianna uses the dining room window." Mac looked at her a little wildly, then took a deep breath.

"Let's go," he said, reaching for the wine and flowers he had brought.

"Mmm," Kate murmured as she pushed open the heavy front door. "Smells like sole Siciliano. That's made with wine and fresh dill, and it's stuffed with crab. Oh, Mac, you'll love it."

Small Mike ran across their path after his kitten, and Kate laughed. "Just another Sunday." She called after him, "Hey, Mike."

"Hey—" Mike skidded to a stop. "You brought *him* again!" His round black eyes grew rounder.

Mac knelt on one knee "Hiya, Mike."

"You wanna see my scratches?" Mike held out a hand crisscrossed with tiny red lines. "Can we make another toy for Gray Cat?" he asked. His eyes were pleading. "He lost the other one."

"Sure." Mac brushed a plump cheek with his knuckles. "Right after dinner."

"Okay, Mac, okay . . ." Mike backed up, then turned around to race to the kitchen. *"Mama!"*

When Mac stood up Kate was hugging her uncle. Tony spoke to Mac over Kate's shoulder. "You like children, eh?"

"Uncle Tony, we just walked in," Kate protested.

"What . . . ?" Tony looked as if he had no idea what he had said. "All I did was ask a question—"

"That's all he ever does." Angelo put one big hand on his father's shoulder, and reached out to Mac with his right. "How you been, Mac? Nice to see you again."

"What . . . !" Tony spoke with his shoulders, his arms. "What did I do?"

Mac shook hands with Angelo, then Pietro, and then the whole family was suddenly there in the hallway. Gina kissed Mac on the cheek when he gave her the wine and flowers. Marianna and Tina waved and called hello from farther back in the crowd.

Tony was still going on. "All I did was ask the man if he liked children."

"Okay, Papa," Marianna said.

Gina took charge at last. "Come along, come along, everybody. The children are hungry."

There was the usual clamor at the table, but now Mac was laughing and much more at ease. Kate was right about the sole, it was fantastic, and there was only one small argument this Sunday. It was between Marianna and Pietro, over the state lottery. It was half in Italian, half in English, and very entertaining.

"He's still buried in the nineteenth century, this one," Marianna finished in disgust.

Kate shook her head. "You know he takes that side to get you mad, Marianna. When he talks to me, he never talks like that."

"It's true." Marianna laughed and tore off a piece of bread. "He thinks it's fun to make me lose my temper. But I have my revenge." No one dared to ask what *that* was. Marianna Sanducci was a twenty-six-year-old second-generation Italian girl, with a master's in psychology and a ninth-month pregnancy. She and Pietro fought loudly and wholesomely about everything from childbirth to earthquakes. But they had been married for four years and were very, very happy.

Kate looked at Mac and wondered if they could love so well. His eyes found hers and she was certain of it.

"So, Mac." Her uncle said the name as if it left a strange taste. "I would not like to ask any personal questions"—he looked around at his family, showing them how persecuted he felt—"but how do you like the fish?"

Mac smiled. "It's the best I've ever had, Mr. Sanducci."

A hand waved in the air. "Call me Tony."

"Tony." Mac cast a quick glance toward Kate.

"Kate's mother made the dinner. She taught Kate how to cook when she was ten years old—"

"Pa," Angelo said repressively.

Tony tossed his hands high. "*Now* what did I say?" But Gina was already by his side with the wine bottle, forestalling any other comments.

"Have some more wine, Tonio." She poured, trying to look serious. There was laughter around the table.

Later, when Mike had taken Mac by the hand and dragged him off to a little boy's secret place, Kate went to find her uncle. He was alone in the den, reading a magazine, his feet up on an ottoman.

"*Zio* Tony," she called softly.

He nodded sleepily. "*Vieni qui, cara,* and close the door."

Kate smiled tenderly and did as she was told.

This man had given her everything; his earnings, his protection, and so much love. Never once had he been too busy for her. "How do you always know when I need to talk to you?"

Tony laughed with a great huff. "I tell you a secret, *carina*. Since you could make the words, whenever you want to talk to me about something very serious—one time it was a kitten, another time you had given a little boy a very big nose— then you call me *zio* in that sweet voice." He shrugged majestically. "It is always the same."

"Oh, *zio*." Kate fell to her knees beside his big chair and put her arms around him. "I love you very much." He didn't answer, he just squeezed her tight.

"Now," he said gruffly as he put her away from him, "you want to talk." He waited, but Kate was having some difficulty with the words. She sat back on her heels and stared at the intricate pattern of the dark Oriental carpet. "Maybe," Tony went on, "you want to talk about your young man?" She didn't look up, but she shook her head. "Maybe . . . you want to talk about your father?" An alarm slammed through her and her gaze shot to his.

He knew.

"I don't know how you thought I would miss a name like Riccardo Ferranti in the newspapers, *regazza mia*, but I did not. I left messages at the museum, and last Tuesday Riccardo called me. You don't look like him at all." Tony's laugh was warm and gritty.

Kate smiled, embarrassed, and held up her hands.

"Ah, *sì*, the hands. You are lucky, Katerina, you might have had his forehead. Riccardo has a very short forehead." Tony laughed again, then swallowed and looked away. "Your father is a good man, Katerina. He was my brother, more than a brother. And you, *regazza*, are my own. I have had you for so many years, I think that I can share you, now."

"*Zio*." She hugged him again, then settled on the wide arm of the easy chair, in a place worn by many small bodies. Tony held her there securely. "How will I tell Mama?"

"I think that I should tell Gina. But Riccardo has asked that I wait until his name is cleared."

"And if that doesn't happen?"

"Always, you are the one to worry. Instead, why don't you tell me about this Adam MacHugh."

Kate covered her face with both hands, then let one eye sneak a look. "Next week?"


She found Mac in the garden with Mike, rolling around on the ground in a fierce wrestling match. When he saw Kate out of the corner of his eye, he collapsed, arms and legs spread wide. But his opponent continued to bounce on his chest without mercy until Mac was forced to recover and retaliate. This time Mike was quick to cry uncle.

There was a faint call from the house and Mike ran off in answer. Mac lay where he was, and Kate let her white skirt billow around her as she sat beside him.

"So, you like children, eh?" She did an excellent Uncle Tony.

Mac smiled wryly as he turned his head her way. "That one wore me out." He let his gaze sweep her face before he looked back at the sky through the branches of the pomegranate tree. "I hope ours look just like you."

Kate felt the blush, but was helpless to prevent it. "It's getting late," she said, pulling at her skirt. "Want to drive up the coast and watch the sunset?"

Mac considered this, putting his hands behind his head. "Can we neck in the backseat?"

"I drive a Volkswagen."

"I'm inventive."

Kate grinned.


They stopped by Kate's house for warmer clothes. It was mid-November, and though the days were still mild, the nights were turning cooler.

Mac had confiscated two drawers and a section of the closet space days ago, and Kate left him to change while she made a thermos of coffee. They crossed paths with a quick kiss in the hallway, and Kate found a soft angora sweater and corduroy trousers in pearl gray while Mac threw together a couple roast beef sandwiches. She pulled her coat and a blanket from the hall closet. Mac met her there with the wicker basket, and they were ready to go.

It took nearly forty minutes to get past Malibu, but from there it was only a short way to Point Dume. Mac drove with one hand on the wheel, the other covering hers on his thigh. Feeling the play of his muscles under her hand satisfied something in Kate that she couldn't explain. But driving like that, touching him so intimately, with the smell of the sea and the changing colors of the day around them, her hair tossed about by the rushing wind—it was good. Very good.

They didn't speak, but Mac caught her staring at him and smiled. That was enough.

Finally, they found the deserted stretch of beach they sought. They parked, and Kate raced Mac down through the ice plants to the sand. They spread the blanket, and when they sat, Mac sheltered her body with the curve of his own so that Kate settled, spoon-fashion, between his legs. He wrapped his arms around her and they gazed at the sky and sea, waiting.

Slowly, it came. The sky paled before it was splashed with the softest pinks, violets, and oranges. When those colors began to darken, Kate stirred in Mac's arms with the drama.

"Oh, look." She pointed as the lines widened, lengthened. "The color . . ." She was awed, as he was by her. "I couldn't be happier," Kate said, her head nestled in the hollow of his shoulder. "I can't imagine being happier than this."

He nuzzled just behind her ear. "I love you, Kate."

Her arms tightened over his. "Has it been years? I feel like I've always known you, that I've always had this, and yet, I'm almost afraid something might happen to take it all away."

"Listen to me, now, Kate," he said quietly. "What we have, I was never even sure existed. Some part of me might have wished for it, but I couldn't have known it could really happen. Now I have it, and there's nothing, *nothing* that's going to take it away from me . . . or you." He leaned closer to kiss the edge of her closed eye. "We're the lucky ones."

"I love you . . ." She twisted to find his mouth with hers. "Love you." His mouth gave her the urgency she craved, the taste of dark desire. One large, callused hand covered the front of her throat, the other held tightly to her hand. Kate made a small sound of need.

His tongue seduced her, teasing at the secrets behind her lips. His hand slipped beneath her coat to her breast, touching her in a way only love can touch, in a way that ached to bring pleasure, that needed a sigh in answer. Kate let her hands run slowly up and down his strong thighs cradling her.

The waves came within ten feet of them, the sky burned more brightly as the sun slid lower. And then, so quickly, it was gone, leaving only muted color. When that turned a dusky blue, Mac wrapped Kate's hair in a rope about one wrist. She turned with the pull, pressing her lips to the warm, rich-smelling skin of his neck. Another tug of her hair, and her head bent back for his kiss. There were many kisses—innocent, affectionate, joyous. And they laughed, for no reason, for all the reasons.

When Kate turned her back to him once more to see the stars, Mac leaned forward to whisper softly in her ear, so softly that it might have been a murmur of the wind.

"What?" She smiled, tenderly, over her shoulder.

"Marry . . . me," he enunciated.

Her body stiffened, and she looked back out at the endless sky, the far reaches of a white-tipped ocean. "Say it again."

"Marry me, Kate." His voice was stronger now, his arms more sure.

She pulled away, right out of his arms. She needed to be face-to-face with him. Sitting on her feet, she reached out one hand to touch his cheek, rough now with a hint of golden-red beard. She pushed back a lock of hair from his forehead. Then she let his green-gold eyes draw her closer, closer, until she could feel his soft breath on her lips. She smiled, brushed his mouth lightly, and asked, "What took you so long?"

He growled and pushed her back to lie flat on the blanket. Impact sent the air from her lungs, and she drew a quick, startled breath. Holding her hands above her head, Mac bent over her and said, "I was waiting for *you* to ask *me* . . ."

# *Thirteen*

It was raining, not a soft drizzling rain, but torrents. Windshield wipers were almost no use, and traffic was slow.

Kate looked at Mac as he maneuvered along the dark, water-slicked boulevard. Her hands pleated the wool of her pants again and again, until she noticed what she was doing.

"You think the rain will be a big problem?" she asked, glancing out the window.

"The outside cameras won't distinguish much." Mac was frowning and kept his gaze straight ahead. "And we're going to get a little wet."

"Where are we supposed to meet my father?" They were near the turnoff now.

"At the van," Mac said automatically. He was preoccupied. Riccardo had called him at four o'clock that afternoon to tell him Guy Jarré had requested the security check from patrol cars, but the time he had given for the request was a full three hours after the shipment's scheduled arrival. Riccardo figured an hour at most for the delivery process. That left two hours. If Jarré was going to break into the warehouse, it would probably be during those two hours.

Kate would watch the monitors in the van while Riccardo's own security team, stationed in and around the building, planned to catch Jarré in the act. If he wasn't caught with goods-in-hand, there was the possibility their evidence would not stand up in court.

Mac turned onto the small street behind Santa Monica. It was lined with parked trucks of every size, but the security van was easy to spot. It was the only vehicle that had no identifying marks. Mac pulled to the curb, parked, and turned to give Kate a quick kiss.

"Ready?" he asked.

She nodded and opened her door. Mac joined her and grabbed her elbow, and then ran through puddles to the gray van. The sliding door opened at their knock, and a hand ushered them inside.

Kate embraced her father, then her uncle. There was one other man inside, and the van seemed very crowded. Mac shook hands all around, then the other man, introduced as Jack, passed Kate a two-way radio.

"This is your 'rover,' ma'am," he said. His accent was South Bronx. "We're all on the same frequency. So, you see anything on these monitors, anything at all, you just press this button and say the number of the monitor. You got that, ma'am?"

"I think so." She was not about to joke with the man. He was deadly serious. "Will you run a test with me?" Jack nodded shortly, but he looked at Kate differently after that. They tested the devices, then checked the time.

Mac decided to stay with Riccardo. Tony would announce any cars turning the corner.

Left alone but for the six television monitors, Kate listened to the thundering of the rain on the roof of the van. The exhibit had been unloaded half an hour ago, but the monitors had shown only her father's own men for the last twenty minutes.

"Nothing yet, Kate?" Mac's voice came over her hand unit.

"My outdoor cameras are still unclear, Mac. But I see no movement." She said the word "no" loud and clear.

"All right, Kate. We'll check in again in five minutes."

She took her finger from the button, and then she saw it. There was a bulky shape, close to the back door. She got within two inches of the screen to make sure. Yes, there was definitely an unaccounted for presence at that door. But the shape? What was he carrying?

She fumbled for the "rover," grabbed it tight, and took a deep breath. "I have something on monitor two, monitor two, Mac."

"Got it," came the short reply

In three minutes the man was inside. Kate waited to announce it. Her hand was getting a cramp. She could see him, but it was still difficult to distinguish exactly what he was carrying. It looked like an oversized backpack. Above Jarré's head, low-beam factory lights were on. He wore dark clothes and gloves, and his hair was plastered to his head. He moved low and quickly, but there would be no doubt who was on the film. The profile was too unusual.

There were ten crates. Jarré went up to the smallest, pulled a piece of metal and a strip of cloth from his bag, and began to pry open the top of the crate. It took only seconds, then he was sifting through the straw. He drew out a figurine, wrapped it, and put it in his bag.

"Mac," Kate said hurriedly into the "rover," "he got a figure from one of the crates. Jade, I think. He's opening another one, taking a shiny piece, something metal. He's got a shoulder bag."

There was a moment's silence, then, "Okay. We're moving, Kate."

It was like watching a movie, or a dream. Kate saw a security man step out from behind a crate. He placed his hand on his holster. Jarré glanced at the man but didn't pause. He took something the size of his palm from his jacket pocket and pulled a pin from it. When he saw Ferranti enter through the front, he switched his aim.

The radio fell from Kate's fingers as she stood too quickly. She pressed her hand flat against the cold television monitor and cried out sharply. She expected a horrible explosion, but instead there was fire and the popping sounds gunshots make.

"No," she shouted, then turned and pushed the sliding van door open. The blinding rain made loud, slapping noises on the tar. She put a hand up to shield her eyes and ran. She stumbled once or twice, but never stopped. She ran down the street toward the warehouse, using the sides of the parked trucks as support.

She was only twenty feet from the warehouse door when she was hit from the side and knocked to the muddy ground. Dazed and short of breath, she was dragged upright by one arm and pushed around the edge of the first truck into the small shelter behind the cab.

Kate looked up into the face of Guy Jarré. He held her arm in one hand, a gun in the other. She struggled hard, stepping down on his instep. But with a curse he put one arm about her neck in a choke hold.

"Quiet, or I break your neck!" he said, giving her a small shake. And Kate was quiet, dragging in precious air, her eyes half-closed against the rain. She would put nothing past the man at this point. His arm tightened as a dark shape ran by only a few feet away, then he pulled her farther back behind the cab.

"We wait," he said, as if to himself. Another man ran past them and he changed his mind. "Your car." He looked down at her. "Where is your car?"

"End of the block," she whispered.

"I have a gun, Kate," he said. His voice was low. She nodded in answer. "I am going to take my arm away, but . . . remember the gun." That charming accent was not quite so charming now. She nodded again, and he slowly pulled his arm away, only to grip her above the elbow. He looked both ways, then pushed her ahead of him into the street.

Kate's heart slammed against the wall of her chest. She had just remembered—Mac had the keys to the car.

The fire had only scorched the outside of two of the crates before Riccardo's men had it under control. Riccardo was holding a handkerchief to his head, where he had bumped it when he jumped away from the incendiary grenade. He was giving orders to one of the men to stay with the exhibit while the others searched for Jarré. Not that it really mattered anymore. They had more than enough evidence on tape.

Mac tried getting Kate on the radio, but there was no response. Again. "Kate, this is Mac, can you hear me?" Something was wrong. Mac headed for the open warehouse door.

He ran with a long stride, across the lawn, following the line of trucks. The sound of his breathing was loud in his ears. In his mind there was only one thought. *If he hurt her . . .*

He found the unmarked van and scanned the

inside from the driver's window. The sliding door was open a few inches. No one was inside. Mac's skin felt cold. Then a hand fell on his shoulder.

He whirled around, ready, only to find Tony behind him, a finger to his lips. Tony pushed him between two trucks and pointed.

There they were.

Jarré had Kate by the arm, a gun in his other hand. They were almost directly across the street and heading for the white Volkswagen.

"Can you get the gun from him if I get his attention?" Tony whispered. Mac clenched his jaw and nodded slowly. "Good. My car is just up the street. Count to fifty, then be ready." Tony backed around the other side of the van and was out of sight. Mac crossed the street twelve feet behind Jarré, moving as silently as he could.

*Thirty.* He could see that Kate's hair had fallen down her back in childish tangles.

*Thirty-five.* Jarré was looking ahead and to the left and right in quick motions. Mac hesitated. In his impatience he was getting too close too fast.

*Forty.* Kate tripped on something and Jarré jerked her forward.

*Forty-five.* Mac could already feel the man's throat between his hands.

*Forty-eight.* Mac's left hand tightened around the two-way radio.

*Fifty.* A car alarm sounded loudly from across the street. Mac saw Jarré's gun hand swing right, following the noise. Mac raised the radio and, in one leap forward, slammed it against Jarré's temple. When the man began to fall, Mac grabbed the gun.

Tony was there almost immediately. He put one foot in the middle of the Frenchman's back, and turned to Mac. *"Bravo."*

His gaze never leaving Kate, Mac placed the gun

on the hood of the Volkswagen. Then he took her carefully in his arms. "Are you hurt, love?" he asked, looking into her eyes. She shook her head no and held him to her.

"Why would he set fire to the very things he wanted?" Kate asked. She was sitting on her couch, wrapped up in a comforter, a snifter of cognac warming in her hands. A fire blazed hypnotically. Mac sat down beside her and held her bare feet in his hands to rub them warm.

"His plan was to take one or two things that wouldn't burn. When the insurance people went through the rubble, those objects would be conspicuous by their absence." His hands moved up to her ankles.

"Implicating my father again."

"Right."

Kate let her head roll, left, right, and around. Mac lifted one hand to massage some of the tension away.

She murmured with appreciation when he got to her shoulders. "What will happen to them, Guy and his wife?" she asked.

"For Jarré, grand larceny, arson, attempted murder, hostage taking. He'll be busy. His wife—who knows what her defense lawyer will say on her behalf?"

"Jarré didn't seem like an evil man," Kate said quietly, thoughtfully. "I used to think you could sense evil in someone. At times I still believe I can. Guy Jarré was a surprise."

Mac kissed her then, to take the bitter taste away.

•   •   •

Gina looked like a girl. She certainly blushed like one. Her blond hair was woven into a perfect French braid. She was wearing a dress the color of her dark blue eyes and he looked down far too often, checking her figure.

She made lasagna that Saturday, three and a half inches thick. She kept herself busy in the kitchen so she would stay far away from the mirrors and the clocks. It seemed everywhere she turned in this house there were mirrors and clocks.

The children were terribly quiet today.

Wasn't there anyone in this house who could make a bit of noise? she wondered.

Mac kept Riccardo busy with five-card stud from five in the afternoon until seven. Riccardo won and was too distracted even to accuse Mac of cheating.

"I think now," Mac said with an *interesting* smile as he dealt again, "would be a cunning moment to ask you for your daughter's hand in marriage."

Riccardo never faltered. "You are, indeed, a wise young man." He stopped fiddling with his cards long enough to say, "Now tell me how much money you make."

It was a beautiful evening, bright and warm with a cool, dancing wind. The sun was just beginning to descend.

Andrew drove, and did not speak. Mac was beside him. He glanced into the back seat, eyebrows rising in signal. Kate acknowledged the signal with a nod.

"Were you ever married, Father?" she asked, using the best distraction she could think of. She could tell Mac wasn't exactly pleased with her choice.

"Yes," Riccardo said, looking her right in the eye. "It was ten years after I was arrested. We had no children. She died. I won't apologize to you, Kate—"

"And I would never ask that." She was sincere, and it was important to her that he know that. "It was your life. I hope you had some happiness in it." Then she put her head down and looked up into her father's eyes. "But it's not over, yet."

He touched her soft cheek. "Thank you, Katerina."

In that moment Kate remembered the sting of every nasty remark directed at a fatherless girl. The looks her mother had suffered through the years. She measured those memories against the future.

She had a father who wanted to know her. After so many years, her parents might have been separated, divorced, or dead. Instead, they were about to meet after too long a time, and were looking forward, not back.

So would she.

No curtain fluttered in the windows of the big house today. Kate pushed open the front door and took her father by the hand to pull him into the hall. Mac and Andrew followed.

Mac breathed deeply of the now familiar scents of Italian cooking. Then he wondered at the lack of sound. Where were the noises of the television and radio, the booming voices of this family?

Kate went right to the heart of the house; the den. Tony was there, reading the evening paper. It rustled loudly as he stood in welcome.

"Good," he said. He held out his arms for Kate, and shook hands with each man. Riccardo was looking around for Gianetta, but she wasn't there.

He exhibited the first sign of nerves Kate had seen.

"She has changed her mind?" he asked. His face was stiff.

"No, no, she is upstairs," Tony hastened to reassure him. "The family will be here in a while. We thought you should have time to talk . . . alone." Riccardo relaxed a bit, but his movements were still awkward. Tony put one hand on his shoulder. "Let me call her." He walked into the hall to the bottom of the stairs. Kate followed quickly and caught his arm.

"I'll get her," she said, and ran quickly up the stairs. The door she wanted was down the hall. She knocked lightly. "Mama?"

"*Si, carina,*" her mother answered.

Kate opened the door. "He's here, Mama, waiting for you." Then she smiled. "Oh, you look beautiful."

Gina was at her old-fashioned vanity. Her blue eyes met Kate's in the large round mirror. There was a soft blush in her cheeks and her eyes shone brightly. "Truth, Katerina. I don't look a hundred years old?"

Kate laughed softly and came close to put both hands on her mother's shoulders. "How can you be so blind? Look." She touched her mother's cheek and pointed to the mirror. "This is a beautiful woman, full of life and love."

Gina's hands covered her daughter's. "But will *he* think so?" she whispered.

Kate stood back, beckoning with a quick wave and a wide smile. "There's only one way to find out."

"So." Gina stood and gave last backward glance. "We go."

"Just one thing more." Kate pulled something from her trouser pocket and placed it carefully in her mother's hand. Gina opened her fingers and gasped. *"La donna di mare*, The Lady of the Sea." The diamonds in the mermaid's hair and tail seemed very bright as Gina blinked quickly. She took a great breath, and gave the necklace to Kate to fasten.

Kate stood at the top of the stairs and watched her father's face as her mother approached him, one of her hands gliding over the cherrywood railing. A warm golden light came from a window on the landing.

There was a dark flush on Riccardo's cheeks as he watched Gina come closer. She was here. "Gia," he said in a bare whisper. At the sound of his voice, she paused for a moment, smiled shyly, and continued down. Riccardo saw the pearl pendant when she touched it with one hand, and he moved forward. His hands reached out for hers as she arrived at the last step.

"Who would have believed you would grow more beautiful?" he said quietly, his words in Italian, for her alone. His eyes caressed the curve of her cheek, her brow, the tiny laugh lines that fanned the clear blue eyes. Then they fell to her mouth, tinted a warm pink. Her lips were parted in excitement. They moved as if to speak, then were still.

He had a beard. It was wonderful on him, Gina thought. The boy was a man. Character was etched into the lines of his face, but with all the charisma of his youth. Then he smiled at her in a way she had never been able to forget.

Her own lips curved. "Rico."

The moment hung in the air, touching each of them. Kate cried, unashamed. Tony, too, found a use for his handkerchief. Andrew shuffled his big feet and shoved his fists into his pockets. Mac's gaze sought Kate.

Tony cleared his throat and stepped forward. "Go, the two of you, into the study." His hands made pushing motions. "In a half hour the family comes, and there is much to say. We will have a glass of wine and wait for you."

"Did Katerina tell you about the first time I saw her?" Riccardo asked Gina as he gave her a glass of sherry.

Gina nodded. "But I would like to hear the way it was for you, Rico."

His head fell back as he looked into a high, far corner of the room. "I was haunted that evening," he said—his voice was music—"as I have been from time to time, by memory. From my terrace I felt the sadness of a beautiful, starry night. I was to attend a party in Bel Air, a silly thing, for which I had no heart. But it was important that I stay in the public eye. There was already enough gossip about the exhibit I was protecting.

"I had almost decided to leave this dull gathering, when I saw a lovely girl across the room. Her face was the face of a madonna, eyes like sapphires. Her hair was honey-gold. Even her form reminded me . . . Gia, it was you. And then she turned and her necklace caught the light. Your pearl." He came to her, taking the glass from her so that he might hold her hands in his once more. His eyes looked black with feeling. "I cannot tell you how I felt in that moment. My mind was spinning. I had no thought at all except that nothing would keep me from that girl. We danced, and I was certain she knew me. There was no doubt that she was yours. But until she told me her name I could not imagine that she was ours. She told me that you were alive, not married." His gaze fell away from hers. "Gia, can you forgive me? We should have been married. You should never have been alone."

Gina smiled tenderly. "We cannot change the past, *caro*. I have been very happy. I went to college. I am a *cordon bleu*. I raised the boys and Katerina—"

"Gia." Riccardo interrupted her sane conversation. "I would like to kiss you."

She looked surprised. "Why do you wait?"

"It's crooked."

"You lie."

Kate turned her head to look at Mac. "I'm telling you, it's crooked."

"My shelves are perfect." He held her more tightly for emphasis. They were lying on the carpet, two pairs of feet pointing toward the new stereo.

"Your strength is impressive," she said, and he loosened his grip. "But you're cock-eyed." She took the lobe of his ear between her teeth. "You can kiss me any . . . way." He took her breath. That mouth, the way he kissed; that tongue, the heat.

She sighed. "I could marry a man who kisses like that."

"You did." His mouth moved down, grazing her throat, her collarbone.

"Oh."

"*Mio cuore*," he said to her shoulder.

"My heart," she translated.

"*Cara*." He buried his face between her breasts.

"Dear one." Her hand was in his hair. He smelled of the wild woods.

"More," he demanded. His hands ran down her ribs to her waist, her hips. She was soft, rosesweet.

She rolled over to lie on top of his broad chest.

*"Bello."* She ran two fingers from his forehead to the tip of his chin.

His laughter rumbled beneath her, and he turned so that she was lying under him. "Beautiful one."

*"Esso . . ."* she began, her hands teasing at his chest.

*"Esso . . ."* he repeated, kissing the side of her neck.

She sighed and took an unsteady breath. ". . . *è storto."*

". . . *è storto,"* he said against her lips. Now she was exactly where he wanted her. "What did I say?"

She closed her eyes and smiled. "It . . . is crooked."

# THE EDITOR'S CORNER

"Jolly" and "heartwarming" are words I don't hear or see nearly enough these days. That's a pity because they're wonderful words ... as well as the perfect ones to describe the quartet of romances we're publishing next month to start off the New Year with warmth and cheer.

In **DISTURBING THE PEACE**, LOVESWEPT #178, Peggy Webb gives us a worthy successor to her intense, yet madcap romance **DUPLICITY**, LOVESWEPT #157. This book is particularly well-titled because heroine Amy Logan, an inventor, truly does disturb the peace of her new neighbor Judge Todd Cunningham. Amy has a few problems perfecting her creations—like an erratic robot named Herman and a musical bed that isn't correctly programed to observe the fine distinctions between night and day. Todd is lovestruck from their first meeting, and Amy is clearly captivated by the sexy judge ... but she is also terrified of the risk he represents. Mistakenly interpreting Amy's resistance to her miscasting of him as a stuffy legalbeagle, Todd sets out to change her image of him. With a bit of assistance from Amy's zany mystery writer aunt and lots of virile charm on his own part, Todd merrily campaigns to win over the imp who has stolen his heart. A sheer delight.

Joan Elliott Pickart really outdoes herself with her next love story, **KALEIDOSCOPE**, LOVESWEPT #179. And in the secondary characters in this book, she creates two of the most delightful ladies it's been my pleasure to meet in a long, long time. Those "ladies" are devoted to liberating themselves from conventional expectations for "older people." They are also the loving mothers of our heroine and hero. Now, when these two formidable matchmaking moms plot to get their offspring introduced to each other, they do

*(continued)*

so in a fashion that sets the kaleidoscope of life swirling with brilliant color. Heroine Mallory Carson is a beauty and hero Michael Patterson is one gorgeous blond hunk of a divorce lawyer. Naturally Michael has seen enough of the miserable side of married life to be turned off even to the words "happily ever after," much less to believe in them. Still, he can't resist Mallory and is even drawn to her day care center, a spot he would find a most awkward one for him if Mallory was not there. Then, when the rainbow colors of love explode before the very eyes of this pair who consider themselves mismatched, they have to take the biggest chance of all.

Don't miss this wonderfully humorous and emotionally moving love story.

Patt Bucheister gives us just what every woman needs in LOVESWEPT #180, **THE DRAGON SLAYER**. She gives us a white knight in Webb Hunter. When Webb falls—literally—on and for our heroine Abigail Stout he soon decides to appoint himself her own special slayer of dragons, bringing her teddy bears and toys . . . and his promise of earth shattering passion. Abigail has been to busy with school and work and more work to have had much experience with men, so she is ill-prepared for the pursuit of Webb, who is as enchanted by her saucy personality and her beauty as he is by her most intriguing perfume: vanilla extract! Abby has learned the hard way (shunted from one foster family to another during her childhood) that happiness is fleeting and dreams do not come true . . . and she is as hard pressed to resist Webb as she is to believe in his promises. Just as you responded to Patt's first LOVESWEPT (**NIGHT AND DAY,** #130) so, too, I think, you will respond with enormous enthusiasm for this touching and memorable romance.

Is there any writer more evocative or imaginative than Fayrene Preston? Her zany cast of characters in

(continued)

**ROBIN AND HER MERRY PEOPLE,** LOVESWEPT #181, will worm their way into your affections just as they do hero Jarrod Saxon's. Heroine Gena Alexander has run from Jarrod whom she is convinced has betrayed her love, her trust. Starting a new life with her merry (but poor) people, Gena's eyes are opened to human suffering and to tragedy, and, like Robin Hood, she determines to do something about them. When Jarrod tracks her down and makes his intentions clear, both are jolted into an awareness of dimensions of each other that are different from any they'd ever even guessed existed. Discovery . . . joy . . . and complications because of the merry band's problems lead to Jarrod's and Gena's deep and rich revelations about the true meaning of love. This is throbbingly sensual and utterly charming romance that we believe you will long remember.

Chuckles and surprises, passion and affection abound to make for *jolly* and *heartwarming* LOVE-SWEPT reading next month. Enjoy!


Warm regards,

Sincerely,

*Carolyn Nichols*

Carolyn Nichols
 Editor
*LOVESWEPT*
Bantam Books, Inc.
666 Fifth Avenue
New York, NY 10103